No More Cornflakes

NO MORE CORNFLAKES

POLLY HORVATH

FARRAR STRAUS GIROUX

NEW YORK

For Arnie,
B. P. F.

No More Cornflakes

October

~~~~~~

A ll week my parents had been pretending they were
rabbits. They were still at it Saturday morning as I sat
behind the funnies and spied on them. When they saw the
mailman come up the walk, they ducked below the living
room windowsill. They do not want him to think they hang
around waiting for him, although they do.

"Oh, Mrs. Rabbit, oh, Mrs. Rabbit, here he comes," said
my father.

"Hide your fuzzy ears and whiskers," said my mother,
giggling.

My big sister, Letitia, came into the room. I beckoned her
over.

"They're at it again," I whispered.

"At what?" she asked in a normal tone. Letitia just won't
play along.

I motioned her closer. Letitia rolled her eyes but joined
me behind the funnies.

"All week long they've been acting weird—pretending to be rabbits, and calling each other Mr. and Mrs. Rabbit."

"So?" Letitia has the gift of understatement. "I'm going to Kathy's house," she called to my parents on her way out.

I put the funnies down and went up to my room. My parents were being strange. Letitia was at Kathy's. My best friend, Doris, was out of town for the weekend. There was no doubt about it, this Saturday was shot.

In the next bedroom I heard Aunt Kate getting up. Mom, Aunt Kate, and their five sisters had grown up in this house. It must have been very crowded. When Grandpa and Grandma died, my mom and dad made some sort of deal with the other aunts for their share of the house, but there was no dealing with Aunt Kate. She had been the one to return home when Grandpa and Grandma got sick. She had nursed them until they died, first Grandpa, then Grandma. A year later she was planning on moving back to Detroit when in barged my parents, bag and baggage. My mom said the ensuing scene was hair-raising. Aunt Kate said she wasn't going to be pushed out of her own home even though she had been on the verge of leaving anyway. My mom said she tried to be more tactful after that, unlike my father, who kept pointing out charming little apartments in the classifieds.

In a way I always secretly sympathized with Aunt Kate after my mom told me this story because I know what it's like when Mom is happy about something and automatically assumes everybody else is happy, too. It really irritated Aunt Kate, I guess. Mom says a man came on the scene at that point, and Aunt Kate liked her new job in Riverside, so she wasn't all that hot to go after all. My mom kept singing around the house, and Aunt Kate kept stubbornly living in her lilac room.

Aunt Kate goes to bed late and never talks to anyone before noon. If she leaves her room at all in the morning, it's to drift about in a fog. If you pass her in the hall, she turns her head. She usually looks as though her mind is elsewhere. I don't know if she is romantically yearning for some lover who jilted her, if she disdains speaking to such a lowlife as myself, or if she was just born with a mind that is focused somewhere else. Sometimes I think it's the latter, because Letitia ignores me in the same way, so I think it may be genetic. With both of them you can get the impression that they're angry with you when, as it turns out, they're not even thinking of you.

Afternoons, Aunt Kate goes in to the newspaper where she works part-time writing restaurant reviews. The rest of the time she writes what my mom refers to as her bloody, gory murder mysteries. My mom is always suggesting to Aunt Kate that she write something "happier." You can practically see the steam come out of Aunt Kate's ears when Mom does this.

"You always know best, don't you?" she snapped as she walked upstairs the last time my mom suggested it. "The worst of it is, I am 'writing something happier,' " she yelled down at her, emphasizing "happier" scornfully.

"Oh, are you? What is it?"

"None of your beeswax, Ada," said Aunt Kate and disappeared down the hall.

I had to giggle when she said this.

Although I've never thought of myself as a cowardly person, I keep my distance from Aunt Kate. But this Saturday, driven by lonely desperation, I felt just reckless enough to go pay her a little visit.

I tiptoed up to Aunt Kate's door and put my ear against it.

I could hear her moving around. Aunt Kate kept a hot plate and a small refrigerator in her room and made her own breakfasts. I closed my eyes, took a deep breath, and knocked.

"Yes?" barked Aunt Kate.

"Can I come in?"

"Is that Hortense?" She had lived with me all my life and she still didn't know my voice.

"Yes," I said, "it's Hortense."

Aunt Kate opened the door and looked down her big, hawklike nose. She is tall and stately with long brown hair that she wears swept up in an old-fashioned pompadour. I wouldn't call her beautiful exactly, but she is striking. It has something to do with the way she carries herself, I think, like she is somebody and you'd better believe it. She was wearing a billowing Victorian nightgown. She never wears the scruffy, moth-eaten old flannel nightgowns like my mom wears.

"Why, Hortense," said Aunt Kate.

"Good morning," I said. It felt lame. "I've come on a very serious matter," I amended.

"Oh, really," said Aunt Kate. She stood aside to let me in. She had set her little round table with a silver coffeepot, a china cup and saucer, a plate of crescent-shaped rolls, and a china pot of jam. No wonder she doesn't want to have breakfast with us, I thought, remembering the plastic dishes we used and that mostly it's Cap'n Crunch and cornflakes.

Aunt Kate moved the chair from her desk over to the table and motioned me to it.

"Some coffee?" she asked. "It's Amaretto, and I happen to have some Devonshire cream to go in it."

"Do you have any orange juice?" I asked.

"It's not polite to ask for orange juice when someone offers you Amaretto coffee. Besides, you know what orange juice tastes like. Have you ever had Amaretto coffee with Devonshire cream?"

"No, but I don't like coffee," I said.

"You don't *know* that, Hortense," said Aunt Kate. "You don't *know* you don't like Amaretto coffee with Devonshire cream because you've never *had* Amaretto coffee with Devonshire cream."

I felt we were off to a bad start. "Okay, I'll try it," I said.

Aunt Kate got another thin, thin china cup and a little plate. She poured me some coffee and put a big spoonful of the thick cream into it. I took a sip. It was awful.

"Have a croissant?" asked Aunt Kate.

I took one of the crescent-shaped rolls and smeared it with jam. It was wonderful.

"I don't suppose we'll ever have these downstairs," I said morosely.

"I don't suppose you will," said Aunt Kate. "Okay, now what's this big, important matter? And it had better be good."

Sometimes Aunt Kate and Letitia sound exactly alike.

"Have you noticed that Mom and Dad have been acting very strangely lately?" I hoped that Aunt Kate considered this good enough, but I had my doubts.

"You mean more so than usual, I suppose?" she asked, nipping at the corner of her croissant.

"Yes," I said, reaching for another croissant. I figured I had better shovel them in while the shoveling was good.

"Well, as a matter of fact, I have," said Aunt Kate.

"All week they've been pretending to be rabbits," I said.

"Yes," said Aunt Kate. "I heard them doing that yesterday."

"And they're always getting together and giggling."

"What do you want me to do exactly?" asked Aunt Kate. "Tell them to stop?"

"No, don't do that," I said. "I've been pretending not to notice. I just thought maybe you knew what was going on."

"Just some silly, temporary game, I've no doubt," said Aunt Kate. "Listen, Hortense, the thing you have to understand about your parents is that they are two very silly people. Sometimes they are sillier than other times. This week they were sillier. Maybe next week they will be less silly. Maybe more. I have been very successful in ignoring them in the past, and I trust I will be equally successful in the future. I recommend you do the same."

This was not the kind of advice I wanted. Worse, the croissant plate was empty. I decided to leave before Aunt Kate forced me to drink any more coffee.

"Well, I guess I'll be going. I have to get to the library," I said, standing up.

"You don't say," said Aunt Kate, pouring herself another cup of coffee and retreating into her fog.

"Well, goodbye," I said, edging toward the door.

"Well, goodbye," she said crisply. The tone in which Aunt Kate repeats what I've said makes me feel particularly stupid.

I went to my room to gather my knapsack and library books. Then I went to get two quarters from Mom for bus fare. She was in the kitchen making a shopping list and acting perfectly normal again.

"Could I have two quarters?" I asked. "I'm going to the library."

"That's a good idea," said my mother, smiling. She bent over to give me a kiss but straightened up suddenly and ran into the bathroom. I could hear her throwing up. When she came back, she looked green.

"Do you have the flu?" I asked.

"No, no," she said with a big, bright, false smile. "I'm fine. Really. Here's fifty cents, plus an extra quarter for the Chocolate Shop. Daddy and I are going grocery shopping, so take your key in case we're gone when you get home."

I thought hard on the way downtown. I didn't like this. I didn't like the big, bright smile. I didn't like my mother going around secretly throwing up. Suppose she was really sick? Suppose she had something *fatal*? "No, don't be stupid," I said to myself. "Would Mom and Dad go around giggling if Mom was seriously ill?" The whole thing was making me intensely nervous. What was this extra quarter bit? Hush money, that's what it was. Extra quarters flowed freely from Daddy, but from Mom—ha!

I went to the Chocolate Shop and bought two red licorice whips. Then I went to the library and looked at all the books and forced myself to take three I had never read so that I could have two Edward Eagers that I had read and reread about sixty times. This was a rule I made for myself because otherwise I would only reread my favorites over and over. I worried that if I didn't make myself read new books, my brain would never progress. I put the books and the licorice whips in my knapsack and went home to spend the rest of the afternoon rereading one of the Edward Eagers and trying to make the licorice whip last four bites to a chapter.

Letitia stayed overnight at Kathy's house and Aunt Kate was eating out, so it was only me and Mom and Dad at dinner. We ate hamburgers and watched TV together. As soon as she had finished her hamburger, my mother went upstairs for a nap. *A nap.* At seven-thirty at night. I had had enough. I went to bed, ate the second licorice whip, and read the second Edward Eager. It was not time for brain progression, it was time for comfort. Good old Edward Eager calmed me down, but it was nip and tuck there for a while.

Sunday morning I got up just in time to throw on my dress and grab a doughnut before being whisked off to church. Last month, when Letitia turned fourteen, she stopped going to church. My parents didn't force the issue. I thought about not going to church, too. I hate getting up early on Sunday morning. I hate the old-candles-burning smell of the church. I don't understand three fourths of the service. It's the longest hour of the week. Still, it makes me sad that Letitia has stopped going. Not that Letitia was so much fun to go with. We used to fight in the back seat on the way there because we both wanted the seat behind Dad.

Now on the way to church, I sit in pristine, lonely splendor in the back seat. Sometimes I can feel our family slipping, oozing into the slough of mediocrity, becoming like those families who never eat together. I'd decided I had better keep going to church for a while yet to maintain a rein on things.

My parents managed to behave themselves in church for the most part except when, just before the service started, my father said to my mother, "That's a nice hat, Ada," and Mom said, "Why, thank you, Mr. Rabbit. I wanted one that was big enough to cover my long and fuzzy ears." And they giggled. *In church.*

After church we drove home to change clothes, pick up Letitia, and go apple picking at the Vermeulen orchard.

Letitia, who had just gotten home from Kathy's, grabbed the bushel basket from the basement. It was already late October and would probably be the last chance this season.

Most of the trees were pretty well picked over and the Vermeulens would be making cider with the rest of the apples soon.

Mom and Dad got in the front seat. Letitia and I hopped in the back. It was a crisp, sunshiny fall day. Dry leaves scuttled on the side of the road. I began to feel that perhaps my family had not gone to seed after all. This was the best time of the year.

We passed the dump and I looked for the buffalo. "Why do they keep buffalo at the dump?" I asked.

"To eat the garbage," said my father.

"Yes, but why buffalo?" I asked.

"You always ask that," said Letitia. "Don't you get tired of asking the *same* question every time we pass the dump?"

"No," I said, "It's the traditional question. Why buffalo?"

"I don't know why, Hortense," said my father. He never seems very curious about this, which is just as well, as I would rather hear people's speculations.

"Maybe it's an all-American dump," said Letitia.

"But," said Mom, giggling, "why not rabbits?"

Everyone was very quiet after that.

We drove into the Vermeulens' drive, then down the rutted lane through the McIntoshes, past the Cortlands, until we came to the Jonathans, which are my mom's favorites. She won't waste her time with any other kind. I like McIntoshes myself, and sometimes I sneak a few into the basket.

My dad pulled the car into the adjacent field and we all jumped out into the long grass. I ran down the rows looking for the perfect tree. I don't pick my apples from just any tree. It has to have beautiful apples and an interesting branch arrangement. When I found a good one, I climbed to the top through the maze of gnarled limbs. This is another test. Some trees rate an A for apples but only a C for climbing. At the top of the tree I ate an apple and beat my chest with my fists, calling "Aaaaaa" like Tarzan. Letitia used to join in this game, but now that she is a teenager she just picks like a common grownup. I pity her. She never has fun anymore. I was watching her sadly when my mother started hopping down the apple rows. Hopping! I wish she'd stop that, I thought, biting into another apple.

"Hey, Hortense!" called a voice.

I froze. It was Virginia Vermeulen. Awful Virginia Vermeulen. She goes around in torn-up-looking T-shirts and jeans, with her hair all wild, and nobody in the fifth grade likes her. She hangs out instead with a bunch of seventh-grade boys.

"Hi," I said, thinking, Get lost.

"That your family?"

"Yeah," I said.

"That your mother?"

"Yeah," I said, trying to play it cool.

"What was she doing?"

I felt sick. If Virginia had seen her hop, she would tell her friends, and then it would be all over school.

"What do you mean?" I inquired casually.

"She have trouble walking or something?"

"I don't know what you mean," I said.

Virginia shrugged and went away. Suppose she went off to hide in a tree and spy on us? Suppose Mom broke into rabbit talk? I swung out of the tree and ran to where my parents were picking.

"If you hop one more time, I will never speak to you again," I said to my mother.

"Us rabbits, we're born hoppers," my mom said.

"Stop it." I fought back tears. "Stop it. Virginia Vermeulen is here. She saw you hop."

My mother looked down at me and her expression changed. "Oh, honey," she said, "we were only playing around."

"Well, it's not funny," I said and ran back to my tree.

Before long the bushel was full and it was time to go home. We stopped at the barn to pick up some cider and grape juice and to pay for the apples. My mom and I avoided looking at each other—it was just easier for us to pretend nothing had happened. Even so, I could see Mom and Dad giving each other meaningful looks.

At home we put the cider on the back porch and the apples in the basement, where they would stay cool for several months. My mom started a pie. Aunt Kate sat at the table eating the apple pieces that Mom was slicing and reading bits from the editorial page of the paper.

I was sitting on the stairs overlooking the kitchen, peeking in on them and eavesdropping.

" 'Why don't these aid-to-the-homeless types just go live in Russia where they would be happier?' " she read. She put the paper down with a disgusted look. "Why do they persist in printing letters from idiots?"

"It's a free country," said my mother with originality. "Besides, it's your paper. I guess that man's got as much right to voice his opinion in it as you do yours."

"Well, as a matter of fact, he hasn't got as much right to his opinion as I do to mine because his opinion is wrong. I wouldn't even go so far as to call it an opinion. That would imply some sort of intelligence at work," said Aunt Kate, lifting an eyebrow and biting into another apple slice.

"Listen, if you want apple slices, cut yourself an apple. I'm trying to make a pie here," said my mother. Then she went into the bathroom and threw up.

When my mother came back into the kitchen, Aunt Kate said, "Don't tell me."

My mother snapped, "Yes, I am."

Aunt Kate put down the paper. "Not again!"

"Three times is hardly call for 'not *again*.' We're very happy about it," said my mother.

"Oh, I dare say," said Aunt Kate. "When are you going to tell people?"

"Well, I thought we'd tell Letitia and Hortense today," said my mother. "Because Hortense has already noticed how sick I am and I don't want her to worry."

I couldn't stand it one more second. I flew down the stairs and into the kitchen. "Tell me what?" I yelled.

"Your mother is pregnant," said Aunt Kate matter-of-factly.

"Oh, shoot," said Mom, wearily wiping her hands on her apron. "I meant to gather the children around my knee and explain that they were going to have a little sister someday. I never can get these scenes right. Something always spoils them. In this case it was *you*," she said turning to Aunt Kate.

"You're going to have a baby!" I screamed. This was really impossible. She was too old. Letitia came into the kitchen and ate an apple slice.

"Letitia," said Mom. "Did you hear what we were saying?"

"Who's going to have a baby?" asked Letitia, sitting on the stepstool.

"MOM!" I shouted.

"*Mom* is going to have a baby?" asked Letitia incredulously.

"Well," said my mother, "I guess you're sort of gathered around my knee now. Yes, along about June you will have a little sister. I just wanted to tell you girls—" she began, but Aunt Kate interrupted.

"Or a little brother," she said.

"Well, naturally it will be a girl," said my mother. "You know that's all Mama had. And that's all her mama had. Why, nobody's had any boys in our family for generations and generations."

"Ada, that's the stupidest thing you've ever said," said Aunt Kate.

"Well, you know it's true," insisted my mom, completely unfazed by anything anyone else had to say on the matter.

"Your odds are fifty-fifty."

"Anyhow, I just wanted to tell the girls that just because a baby is coming—" she began again.

"Is that what all the rabbit jokes are about?" asked Aunt Kate.

"No," said my mother coldly. "Henry and I just finished reading *Watership Down*. Not that it is anybody's business."

"I'm sure I don't want it to be my business, but you've rather forced the issue," said Aunt Kate.

My dad wandered in.

"They know," said my mom dramatically.

"Well, what do you think?" asked my father.

"I think—" began Aunt Kate, but Dad interrupted her.

"I didn't mean you. I meant the girls."

"Good-oh," said Letitia. I guess she's been watching a lot of *Masterpiece Theatre* lately.

"Well, anyhow, I'm glad Mom isn't seriously ill or anything," I said. "But aren't you a little old for this?"

"Apparently not," snapped Aunt Kate.

"Will you quit interrupting," said my father.

"Actually, honey—" started Mom.

"*I* may be too old for this," said Aunt Kate. "Two o'clock feedings again."

"You won't be giving them," said Dad.

"I might as well be," said Aunt Kate. "You know I never could sleep through them."

"You know what you can do about that," said my father.

"Let's all be nice," pleaded Mom.

"Oh, all right," said Aunt Kate. "Congratulations, Ada. I have a lunch date." She swept out.

Letitia stood up. "Oh, my gosh," she said. "I almost forgot, I promised I'd meet Kathy at the tennis court. I'm supposed to have dinner at their house. You don't mind, Mom, do you?"

"Of course not," said my mother. "Just be home at a reasonable hour."

"Can I tell Kathy?"

"Let's wait a bit," said Mom.

"Gee, a little sister," Letitia said as she was leaving.

Dad winked at Mom and went down to the basement.

I felt embarrassed alone with her. I don't like sentimental scenes. Particularly not with my mom. I thought I would say something, but what I wanted to tell her was that she should have asked my advice before starting all this. Also, I knew it hadn't occurred to her that I would be anything except overjoyed at the news. I didn't want any reaction to show on my face.

"Shoot," said Mom. "I never did get to make my big speech."

The doorbell rang and she went to usher in our next-door

neighbor. I could hear them laughing and gossiping in the living room.

I sat by myself in the kitchen and ate pie dough. I had to keep reminding myself that at least she wasn't terminally ill. Nevertheless, this would take some getting used to.

November

~~~~~~

W ell, that's it! It happened, just as I feared! We stopped eating together! We were definitely on the downside from happy human family to beasts in the field.

As the weeks slipped by, Letitia ate at Kathy's more frequently, or skipped meals altogether while she dieted. With just me and my dad to cook for, Mom began to pop TV dinners into the oven. She said she had lost her appetite. I thought this was very unhomemaker-like, but didn't want to mention it to her. I began to suspect that she was going to get awfully wrapped up in this baby-to-be.

When Thanksgiving rolled around I begged my faithful friend Doris to eat with us rather than help her parents deliver food baskets to the needy. I thought this would at least ensure that Mom wouldn't just cook a few Swanson turkey dinners.

Doris and I have been friends since kindergarten. One day her mother called my mother to say Doris wanted me to come over and play. I never understood why Doris of the gleaming white knee socks and symmetrical barrettes picked me and my skinned knees out of the whole kindergarten class. Her prim ladylike ways have always held a strange fascination for me.

Doris sat next to me at the dining room table. We had plates heaped with identical Thanksgiving fare, except Doris didn't have any cranberry sauce because she only likes the jellied kind, and I didn't have any Brussels sprouts. I don't know why my mother even bothers to make them, since who wants to bother with vegetables with all the food at Thanksgiving? Particularly second-rate vegetables like Brussels sprouts. Even those benighted souls who put them on their plates rarely eat them.

I had taken to seeing how long it took before my mom looked sick.

"She's made it past the potatoes," I whispered to Doris.

Doris hadn't eaten at my house since she heard the news, but I had informed her of the little mealtime dramas.

"She's made it past the stuffing," I whispered.

If Aunt Kate had been there, she probably would have made us quit whispering, but Aunt Kate was having dinner with her two strange friends I have named Crony One and Crony Two. Crony One is tall, with very curly hair that is too red to be true. Crony Two is short and fat, with short black hair and a bulbous nose. I don't think either of them is very bright. I have always wondered why Aunt Kate hangs out with them. My mom invited them all to eat with us, but thankfully Aunt Kate said she'd rather be torn apart by rabid dogs.

My mother shuffled food around her plate and looked green. Letitia carefully cut her white meat into teeny tiny bites and asked Mom how much butter she had put in the mashed potatoes. Letitia was on her fourth diet that week. Dad kept glancing over at the clock because he wanted to watch the football game when it came on.

"Do you remember how we all used to get up early and clean the house together Thanksgiving morning?" I said. "Letitia and I would play with the turkey." Letitia and I used to give the turkey a back rub. We felt it was the least we could do, considering how it was going to spend the rest of the day. "And then you would stuff it and make cranberry sauce in the big old meat grinder. We'd all watch the Macy's parade together. At dinner we would say what we were most thankful for. I'm most thankful—"

"What's for dessert?" asked Letitia.

"Pumpkin pie and mincemeat pie, what else?" I said.

"Only pumpkin this year, I'm afraid," said Mom.

"You didn't make mincemeat?" I wailed. "But you know my favorite pie is mincemeat, and we only ever have it at Thanksgiving."

"I don't know why you made any pie," said Letitia. "Everyone in this family is too fat, anyway. Do you know that excess amounts of fat increase your risk of not only heart disease but also cancer? You wanna die of cancer, tubbo?" she asked, turning to me. "I thought if you were going to make any dessert, Mom, it would be the no-cal mousse I gave you the recipe for."

My mother sighed. "I didn't have time for the no-cal mousse, and I will make the mince pie for Christmas, Hortense. It just seemed silly to make two pies with Letitia dieting and Aunt Kate eating at a restaurant."

"I'm most thankful for—" I tried again.

"Ball game!" shouted Dad.

"Go ahead, dear," said Mom. "I'll bring you some pie and coffee in the den."

"You don't have to do that, you know," said Letitia as Dad ran to turn on the game.

"Do what?" asked Mom.

"Bring him his pie and coffee like a slave. He's got two hands, doesn't he?"

"I don't see what business it is of yours, Letitia, if I want to bring him his pie and coffee."

"It's all women's business. You're perpetuating an archaic system."

"Sometimes you sound just like your Aunt Kate."

"Well, there are worse ways to sound."

My mother sighed.

"I guess nobody cares what I am most thankful for," I said bitterly.

"Sure we do," said my mother. "What are you most thankful for?"

"I'm most thankful for my new bike," I said.

"Oh, my gosh, you are so shallow," said Letitia. "Can I be excused?"

"Why don't you stay at the table a little longer," said Mom. "It *is* Thanksgiving."

"You excused Dad," said Letitia.

"All right," said Mom. "Poor Doris, you must think we're a bunch of barbarians."

"Not at all," said Doris politely.

My mother went to get the pie. She cut Doris and me a slice each and then looked ill and left the room.

"She didn't make it past the pie," I said.

"You know what it is," said Doris, taking a tiny mouthful and chewing it carefully, "little sisters are such awful beasts they start making trouble even before they're born."

"You have to think back to what it was like having a baby in the house," I said.

"But that was five years ago," said Doris.

"You were old enough to remember. Don't you remember your mom being pregnant?"

"I don't think I knew she was pregnant. I think I just thought she was fat."

"You couldn't have been that stupid," I insisted. "I knew you then. I would never have been friends with you if I thought you were that stupid."

"Well, you were there. Do you remember my mom being pregnant?"

"I guess not." I sighed. "I just remember making pictures for her when she was in the hospital."

Doris and I had three pieces of pie each. Doris didn't want the last piece, but I insisted. That didn't leave much pie for anyone else, but it served them right.

"Listen, Doris," I said, hiding the remains of the pie in the fridge, "let's go over to your house and play with your paper dolls."

Doris has a much more extensive paper doll collection than I have. She keeps them in a game closet that she shares with her nasty little sister. That's how organized Doris's family is.

"Mom and Dad and Harmony are still out delivering baskets to the needy," said Doris.

"So what?" I asked.

"Mom doesn't like me to stay alone in the house."

"You won't be alone, stupid, because I'll be there," I said.

"You know what I mean. She or Dad or the baby-sitter have to be there."

Doris is my best friend and so, of course, I hate to criticize her, but one of her more unfortunate qualities is her tendency to accept passively anything her parents call for. Her mother is overly protective and needs Doris to rebel to make her see the light.

"If your mother told you to jump off a bridge, would you?" I asked her.

"I doubt if my mother would ever ask me to jump off a bridge, Hortense," said Doris. "Why don't you come over tomorrow for lunch and then we can play with my paper dolls? I will have to ask my mother, of course."

"Of course," I said sarcastically, but it rolled off Doris's back.

Lunch with Doris means lunch with Doris's family. They all sit at the kitchen table, even Doris's father. They always eat something hot, too. The last time I was there, her mother asked me how I felt about enchiladas. Well, the fact was I didn't feel any way about enchiladas because I had never had one, but to be polite I said enchiladas were delightful. So she got out a jar of these things. Everyone got two. Her father put a molded Jell-O salad, crackers, and a piece of cheese on the table. The crackers were arranged on the plate, and the cheese was in a nice chunk with even edges, not the gnawed-off-by-a-bunch-of-rats look that our cheese always has. Aunt Kate would have approved, I am sure. We all sat down and, as usual, Doris's parents tried to engage me in conversation. It was very civilized. Everyone used napkins. At our house those squishy, disgusting-looking enchiladas would have been so much pig fodder. But Doris's mother makes everything look so pristine that I didn't mind them. I felt especially ashamed of the bologna sandwiches Doris and I make for ourselves when she has lunch over at my house.

For dessert we had Doris's mother's homemade molasses cookies. I could eat about two dozen, but I am always very polite and eat only two. You can't even sneak another one later, because Doris's mother puts them back in the cookie jar after lunch. It never occurs to Doris to go into the cookie jar. Sometimes you gotta wonder about her.

These cookies are a real mystery. They are big, dark, and flat and they have sugar and cracks on the top. I made my mother get the recipe, but hers never come out big, dark, and flat, with sugar and cracks on the top. They always come out like little brown mounds and don't even taste the same dark, rich way.

Letitia and I used to bake together every Wednesday night. Thursday morning usually found us pretty sick. We tried, without luck, for three consecutive Wednesdays to get those cookies to come out like Doris's mother's. So, I have to ask myself, is Doris's mother the type who would give you the recipe wrong so that only she and her family get the dark, rich, flat cookies with the sugar and cracks on top? If so, she is wasting her time, because Doris, not being the kind of girl who would sneak into the kitchen after her bedtime to get one more cookie, is unworthy of such a sacrifice of morals. I know, because I suggested stealing a cookie to her the last time I slept over there. Do you know what she said? She said she had just brushed her teeth.

Anyhow, after a Thanksgiving meal like we had, I long for the order of Doris's house even if I think they take it too far sometimes.

We took our plates into the kitchen. My mom came out of the bathroom and sat down at the kitchen table. She looked like a mess. I must say that since she started this pregnancy, she has certainly let herself go. Her hair was all sort of wadded up around her head. Doris's mother has a perm. She looks like she's waiting for VE Day, but at least she is neat.

"I guess I had better get started on these dishes," Mom said. "Letitia!"

Naturally, Letitia was on the phone. Whenever there is anything to be done, you can count on Letitia's being on the phone.

"It's Hortense's turn," Letitia screamed downstairs.

Do you think anyone ever screams in Doris's house? Not likely.

"Hortense has a *guest!*" screamed my mom.

I should think so.

"Oh, all right," yelled Letitia.

She came swishing wearily down the stairs with half her toenails painted purple. Mom won't let her wear fingernail polish but does let her wear toenail polish because she figures no one can see it and know how depraved Letitia really is.

"I was painting my toenails. And look," she said to me, "you made me botch it. Now I'll have to start all over again."

"Come on," I said, pulling Doris away from all these unpleasant people. "Let's go up to my room and cut out furniture from the Sears catalogue." This is how we furnish the paper dolls' houses.

"I can't believe you still play with paper dolls," said Letitia.

The doorbell rang. It was Doris's family, and I could only

hope they hadn't overheard any of the uncouth goings on.

My mother invited them in, and Dad poked his head out of the den.

"Stewie, Marie," he called. "Stewie, catch any of the game?"

"No, not yet," said Doris's father. "Not that I'm such a football fan. Golf's more my game."

"You don't say," said my father.

"Come in and sit down," said Mom.

I didn't know if she meant my father or Doris's parents. Stewie and Marie (as I thought of them, though naturally I called them Mr. and Mrs. Gunderson out loud) and Harmony took off their coats.

"Can I get you some pie?" asked my mother.

"That would be lovely," cooed Doris's mother. "We didn't really have time for a Thanksgiving meal, so we stopped at Knapper's restaurant. They put together quite a nice little turkey dinner, actually."

Harmony sat on the edge of the couch and kicked it rhythmically.

"Henry, would you like some pie?" Mom asked Dad.

I knew she was trying to get him to come all the way into the living room instead of just hanging there in the doorway.

"Want to catch a few minutes of the game, Stew?" he asked hopefully.

"No, thanks," he said. "But you go ahead."

"No, ah, haruum," said my dad, which is what he says when he can't think what to say, and went to sit on the couch.

Just then Aunt Kate and the Cronies, Barbara and Elise, walked in. My father invited them to sit down with us and have some pie.

"Why, thank you," Aunt Kate said. She was stuck.

Cronies One and Two smiled their vacuous smiles and twiddled their thumbs as Aunt Kate introduced them to the Gundersons.

"Hortense, dear, can you come help me?" called my mother from the kitchen.

I went with sinking heart.

"Hortense," she whispered, "did you and Doris eat all this pie?"

"You might say that," I said, hedging.

"Well, what am I supposed to serve everyone out there? Do you expect a miracle like the loaves and fishes?"

"I didn't know everyone was going to suddenly show up and demand pie," I said.

My mother rolled her eyes. She got out plates and started to cut wafer-thin pieces of pie. Luckily, there was a lot of whipping cream, and she put on huge mounds of this, trying to obscure the measly pie pieces. On Dad's plate there was all whipping cream and no pie. We took it out, being careful to give the biggest pie pieces to Stewie, Marie, and the Cronies. They acted like nothing was wrong, but I watched them carefully and could see them furtively hunting for pie.

My dad, who was busily scraping away his whipped cream, said, "Hey, where's the pie? All I got was whipped cream!"

Mom blushed. Aunt Kate made a snorting noise. Mom started giggling so hard she had tears coming down her cheeks. Of course, she had to explain what had happened, and Doris's parents made little laughing sounds, but I could tell they didn't think it was funny at all.

Letitia drifted dreamily into the living room. As usual, I couldn't tell if she was bored by us or was simply thinking of other things. She sat down on the piano bench and made wan half-smiles in the direction of Stewie, Marie, and Harmony after nodding at the Cronies, who were busily scraping their plates to the bone.

"Why, hello, Letitia," said Mrs. Gunderson. "How are you enjoying junior high this year?"

"Fine," said Letitia.

"Well, Stewie, how about those Wolverines?" said Dad. You could tell his mind was still on the game.

"Why don't you ask Mrs. Gunderson about the Wolverines?" asked Letitia, coming suddenly awake the way she and Aunt Kate do.

"What do you mean?" asked Dad.

"How come you asked Mr. Gunderson but you didn't ask Mrs. Gunderson about the Wolverines? Do you assume that just because Mrs. Gunderson is a woman, she isn't interested in football?"

"Why don't you take the dirty dishes back to the kitchen?" suggested Dad.

"I'll help," said Mom and Aunt Kate a trifle too enthusiastically.

It suddenly occurred to me that Mom, Dad, and Aunt Kate didn't like Doris's parents. They were always polite to them, but it seemed they couldn't wait to escape.

Letitia was determined to strike a blow for women.

"Mrs. Gunderson, aren't you interested in football?" she went on, ignoring Dad.

"I can't say that I am, not awfully," she said. "Aren't you just thrilled about having a little baby brother or sister on the way?"

"Sister," said Mom automatically, coming back into the room.

That was Mrs. Gunderson all over. She spends her whole life smoothing things over and changing the subject. She's

an extremely moral woman. That's why I was surprised that
Aunt Kate and Mom and Dad don't like her. What was the
good of being extremely moral if everyone didn't like you?

"I'm terribly excited," said Letitia enthusiastically. "I think
it will be a real boon to my parents, especially with Hortense
and me getting older. Gives them something to occupy their
minds in their sunset years."

Everyone laughed except me and Aunt Kate. The Cronies
just kept looking around the room like they were planning
on redecorating it. Once Crony One said, "How nice," but
no one could tell what it was in reference to, and Aunt Kate
threw her an evil look.

Finally the Cronies left, followed shortly by the Gundersons. I could see Harmony pulling Doris's hair in a sneaky
way. I knew Doris would deal with her later. She couldn't
say anything in front of Stewie and Marie because they always
sided with Harmony. I saw this as just one of the many perils
ahead.

When they were gone, Letitia and Aunt Kate drifted out.
Dad raced back to his football game. I helped Mom finish
the dishes Letitia had started.

"When do you think you'll stop throwing up?" I asked her.

"Oh, I don't know. It depends. When I had you, I was
never sick. But, boy, was I ever sick with Letitia."

"It figures," I said.

"Probably in January," she said.

I wiped the last plate and went to my room. This Thanksgiving had been a bust. We had been together, but we hadn't
been. Everybody was busy with their own concerns. Even
when I talked to my mom these days, her mind was somewhere else. Letitia was too busy doing teenage things to do
family things. I sat on the floor in my room and felt sad.

Even though the Gundersons hadn't had dinner together, I bet they were doing something together tonight. Probably popping corn and watching TV.

I was suddenly very lonely. I went to Aunt Kate's room and knocked on her door.

"I am very busy," she called. I could hear her typing. She was probably writing a review.

"Can I come in anyway?" I called.

"No," said Aunt Kate.

"Please," I said.

She appeared at the door and put one hand on her hip. "Well?" she asked in a way that made her sound just like the Wicked Witch of the West.

"I'm lonely," I said.

"In this house?" she shrieked. "I only wish I were so afflicted."

"I guess I thought maybe you might be lonely too," I said.

"Really?" said Aunt Kate. "Listen, Hortense, I have a column that has to be written by tomorrow. Now, if you are lonely, I advise you to find a project to keep you busy. Busyness is the best cure for loneliness."

"I thought people were the best cure for loneliness," I said.

"People are not the best cure for anything," said Aunt Kate. "Now scram." And she closed the door.

I thought about what she said, and it was true. After all, I had a best friend, but I was still lonely. Aunt Kate had Cronies One and Two, but she didn't look like she had much fun with them.

It was true that I had originally gone to see Aunt Kate because I was in a state of lonely desperation, but she had surprised me by being less formidable than I expected. I detected spots of warmth here and there. For instance, she had told me to scram, but on the other hand, she had given me some sage advice about people. Suddenly, it was a challenge to make her like me. Maybe I could think of such an astonishing project that she would be knocked off her feet. I decided to give it some serious thought.

December

~~~~~~

I tried to think of a big, absorbing project for the next few days, but I kept getting sidetracked by Christmas. My budget being what it is, I am stuck making most of my Christmas presents or doing extra chores around the house to earn some money to buy them. I was scrubbing the downstairs bathroom one Saturday, while next door Mom cleaned the kitchen. You still couldn't tell that she was pregnant, but she kept patting her stomach anyway.

"Did you do that when you were pregnant with me?" I asked her, coming into the kitchen.

"Do what?"

"Pat your stomach."

"Was I doing that?" she asked.

"You do that a lot," I pointed out.

"Funny, I don't remember," she said, scouring the sink. "You forget so much about the pregnancy after you have the baby."

"What *do* you remember about being pregnant with me?"

"Oh, I don't know. I remember chasing after your sister. She was a real handful."

"That's it?" I asked in disgust.

"Well, it's not like I took notes, Hortense."

"But didn't it ever occur to you that I might want to know?"

"I guess it didn't," said my mom, wiping off a counter unconcernedly. Then she sat down to a big bowl of cornflakes. We always eat a lot of cornflakes in our house. We try to eat a lot of cereal generally. Cereal making is a big industry not too far from us, so that it's sort of a point of pride. But since Mom has been pregnant, she's been scarfing up the old cornflakes like nobody's business. It was fascinating to watch her eat. She concentrated so hard on those cornflakes it was like she and they were one. I bet you that in a year she wouldn't remember it, and when this baby got older and asked what it was like when Mom was pregnant, Mom would say, "It's not like I took notes."

It occurred to me that I should keep a record of all the stupid things Mom was doing. I could write down what a jerk Letitia was being. Naturally, if anyone performed a golden deed I would make a note of it, too. I hurried to finish scrubbing the bathroom, and then, deciding Christmas presents would have to wait, I took the dollar I made and went downtown and bought a green notebook at Walgreen's. On the inside I wrote: MY SECRET OBSERVATIONS. I organized it into four sections, one for each person in my family.

Just getting started on a project made me feel in control of things. It also gave me an excuse to go knock on Aunt Kate's door. She was home for once. Usually on Saturday nights she goes out with Cronies One and Two. They go to

bars where there is country music. You'd think that anyone
that heavily into pâté de foie gras would also be into string
quartets, and you would be wrong. I wanted to ask her what
happened to Crony One and Crony Two, but one look at
Aunt Kate's piercing blue eyes and I was a dithering idiot.

"Still lonely, are we?" she asked. She was wearing her
billowing Victorian nightgown and carrying a thick book in
her hand.

"Your nose sounds stuffy," I said.

"I have a cold," she said and sneezed.

"Would you like me to get you an aspirin?" I asked help-
fully.

"What do you want, Hortense?"

"I think I have discovered a project. Can I come in?"

"All right," said Aunt Kate. "But let's not start to think of
this as your hangout."

"Oh," I said, feeling unjustly wounded.

"So?" she asked. She sat at her table and sipped at a steam-
ing mug. On a plate in front of her was half of a processed-
cheese sandwich.

"You're eating processed cheese!" I shrieked in delight.

She grabbed me by the collar and said in the scariest voice
imaginable, "Don't you ever breathe a word of this to anyone!"

I wasn't sure if she was kidding, but I promised not to and
she relaxed her grip. Sometimes I think everyone in my
family is crazy.

"Gee, I like processed cheese myself," I said, rubbing my
neck.

"I do not find that comforting, Hortense," she said.

She kept sipping her hot drink and not offering me any
refreshments the way she had before.

"I think I have a project," I said.

"That's nice," said Aunt Kate. I don't think she was paying any attention to me.

"The question is: Is it the right project?"

"I don't follow," said Aunt Kate.

"Let's say that I am sort of writing a thing. How do I know that this is the right project for me? Do you have a project?"

"Yes. I am writing a book about the cuisine of Lower Michigan."

"You've always written murder mysteries before. How do you know this is the right project for you?"

"If it's a big, absorbing project, then it will run away with you as a fish when hooked properly will run away with the line. If it's not the right project, then it will slip off the hook and you'll have to drop your hook back in and try to catch something else."

"I guess I am sort of at the worm-digging stage," I said.

"I really think this metaphor is getting too cute for me, Hortense," said Aunt Kate.

Well, really! It was *her* metaphor. I felt rebuffed and stood up with dignity. I wanted to say something nasty and cutting, but Aunt Kate's disdainful air was daunting. Instead, I walked out stiffly.

Back in my room, I sat on my bed and stared at the crack in my ceiling. I lay down but I couldn't sleep. Letitia dismissed me, Aunt Kate was abrupt with me, and Mom had apparently *forgotten* me. I took out my green notebook and wrote down my first secret observation. It was about Aunt Kate. It was not flattering. "Just think," I wrote at the end, "while she is writing about restaurants, I am writing about her."

*   *   *

All time is supposed to be the same, but I have observed that this is not the case. December is one of your faster months. The three weeks of school whiz by, and then you are on vacation.

I love the preparations for Christmas. We have a big box of Christmas decorations that I drag out as soon as Mom lets me. Letitia says that the stuff I like to put on the tree, like the paper candy canes that I made in second grade, and the head of the stuffed caterpillar that I used to play with, and the popcorn that I string, is tacky. She wants an artificial silver tree with only blue ornaments. That kind of tree sounds like the loneliest thing in the world to me.

My dad and I shop for the Christmas tree together. We are very particular. When we have found a good one, and decorated it, we turn off all the lights in the room and watch its lights twinkle.

Also, Dad and I put all the special Christmas decorations around the house. We have Santa candles that we never burn—they go in the windows. There is a miniature village that goes in the living room window. The brass carrousel that twirls around when you light a candle in its center goes on the coffee table. It always seems like magic to me. My dad and I just love it. He lies on the couch in the evening by the lighted Christmas tree, and I sit on the floor by him with my paper dolls, and together we watch the carrousel go around.

It's not that Mom, Aunt Kate, and Letitia don't like Christmas. It's just that they don't get that special glow that Dad and I get. I think if we put the miniature village in the den window instead of the living room, they wouldn't mind at all.

Christmas morning we got up and there were tacks in

Letitia's and my stockings. I hardly knew what to make of this. I knew what coal in your stocking was supposed to mean, but tacks? At any rate, as a stocking stuffer, it left me cold. It turned out to be okay because Dad had made Letitia and me bulletin boards for our rooms, and so then the tacks made perfect sense. That was my best present because it gave me an idea. Letitia had warmed up for Christmas—we had even baked Christmas cookies one Wednesday night—but after, and I mean immediately after, she went back to spending all her free time with Kathy and ignoring me completely. One night, in desperation, I got out my sealing wax and my stationery and wrote Letitia a note.

"Dear Fat Hips," I wrote, because Letitia is always complaining about how fat her hips are. "How many Californians does it take to screw in a lightbulb? Signed, Hortense."

I sealed it with my sealing wax and stuck it on her bulletin board. The next night I found a pink note sealed in purple on my bulletin board. It said: "Dear Medusa, How many?"

I knew that Medusa was this very ugly woman with snakes for hair.

I was glad that Letitia didn't know the punch line because it was the most sophisticated joke I knew and I figured it would impress her.

"Dear Fat Hips," I wrote. "One to screw it in and six to experience it. Haha. Signed, Medusa."

I sealed it with wax and stuck it on her bulletin board.

After that I didn't feel like writing such nasty things about Letitia in my secret observations. I turned my attention instead to Aunt Kate. She had been with us Christmas morning, but the rest of the holidays she kept going out with Cronies One and Two.

"How come Aunt Kate never got married?" I asked Mom one day.

"I don't know. I guess she never met anyone she wanted to marry."

We were in the kitchen together and Aunt Kate was loading things into the trunk of her car.

"Why don't you ask her why she's going up north?" I asked.

"If Aunt Kate wanted us to know what she was doing, she would tell us," said my mother, breaking eggs into a bowl and peering into the cookbook.

"Aren't you the least bit *curious*?" I asked in exasperation.

"For heaven's sake, Hortense," said my mother, "don't you have anything to do? Why don't you call Doris?"

"She's visiting relatives *again*," I said.

"Well, call one of your other friends."

"I don't have any other friends," I said. I like having one good friend and that's it. Too many friends, and your life just gets all cluttered. Doris and I are like a nice old comfortable pair of shoes.

"Laurie Cooper?" asked Mom.

"Blech," I said.

Laurie Cooper, who lives down the street, wants to be my friend. She doesn't seem to care that I keep rebuffing her. She has had a doglike devotion to me since kindergarten. I could bear this, but she keeps forgiving me for not liking her.

"Why don't you call that Vermeulen girl?" asked Mom.

"VIRGINIA VERMEULEN?" I shouted.

How little my mother knows of the world. She stopped beating the batter and put her hands on her hips.

"DON'T SHOUT," she shouted. "What in the world is the matter with that?"

"She's a tramp. *Everyone* knows that," I said.

"Hortense Hemple!" said Mom in *that* tone. "Don't you ever let me catch you saying something like that again." Then she calmed down. "What makes you say that, anyway?" she asked offhandedly, but with increasing interest, I could tell.

"She hangs out with seventh-grade boys," I said and stuck my finger in the cake batter.

"Oh, for heaven's sake." Mom snorted. "Get your hand out of the batter."

She made shooing motions with her apron, so I put on my coat and boots and walked out to the car, which Aunt Kate was brushing.

"Where are you going?" I asked, leaning against the car door.

"Up north."

"How about taking me with you?" I asked. "I'd be good company."

"Thank you, but I don't think so," said Aunt Kate briskly. "Barbara and Elise are coming."

"You know, I am really thinking hard about a project to organize this family," I said, stalling for time.

"Oh, really?" said Aunt Kate, arranging fishing gear in the trunk.

"Are you going fishing?" I asked.

"Ice fishing."

"Well, we could start with the laundry," I went on, making it up as I went along. "You know how everyone is always losing socks? Never both socks, just one sock?" I said, wondering what I would say next.

"Listen, Hortense," said Aunt Kate, "I am sick and tired of people always worrying about their missing socks. *My* theory is that we all lose half our apparel in the wash, but you are only alerted to *socks* because the mate shows up. North

Americans own too many clothes. We have so many that we don't even remember what we own half the time, and therefore aren't even aware of all the pants and shirts that go astray. We should all have just one muumuu and maybe a pair of sandals."

"Oh, yeah, how are you going to go ice fishing in that?" I demanded.

Aunt Kate just looked at me.

"Anyhow," I continued, "I suggest we all go downtown together and buy just one color of socks each. For instance, you buy just red socks, Mom buys just green socks, etc. It will make the sock sorting easier, for one thing, and if you lose a red sock, so what? Pair it with another red sock."

"You mean put a lone red sock with a pair of red socks?"

"Right," I said.

"For those days when I go out with three feet."

"Eventually you'll lose another sock, of course. Then you can pair the two odd socks. The important thing is that we *all* do it so that we have everyone color-coded. Afterward we can go for banana splits."

"Wearing our color-coded socks."

"Exactly!" I nodded.

"Goodbye, Hortense," said Aunt Kate, getting into the car.

That night I went up to my room and wrote in my green notebook: "I am going to have to think a lot faster if I want to impress Aunt Kate. Every night I shall do two brain exercises. Does the library have a book on the subject? WHY IS EVERYONE SUDDENLY SO BUSY?"

January

I would really hate January if it weren't for my birthday. January is actually a pretty good month to have your birthday in, and the reason is it helps beat the post-Christmas depression. You know, after anticipating all the good presents you should get, and then getting a nice little pile of neat gifts and the usual percentage of underwear, the whole thing is over for another year. But wait—what is on the horizon? More presents! And better yet, they're *all for you*! Also, if you play your cards right, a cake and your favorite things to eat.

If it just wasn't such a blue and icy month. Icicles hung from our roof, ice covered our walk, the people next door had an ice rink. Everywhere you looked: ice.

Doris and I were sitting at the kitchen table. Letitia was on the heat register. Hot air comes up and it feels good until the register becomes too hot. Then the air gets cold, then it starts up hot again. When she is home, you can catch Letitia bouncing on and off it.

Doris and I were doing our math homework. Everything is a breeze for me at school except for arithmetic, and wouldn't you know it, my teacher just loves arithmetic. Also, wouldn't you know it, Doris just loves arithmetic, so she and the teacher love each other. Now, to tell the truth, I have always been the teacher's pet in years past. Probably because I like to read and write and almost always charm the teachers with my enthusiastic responses to their searching questions. But this year I had to relinquish the role to Doris and a boy in our class who doesn't even know what in Xanadu did Kubla Khan.

This January found me sitting at the kitchen table for too many hours trying to figure out story problems with Doris breathing down my neck.

"The problem is," I said to Doris, "that I get sidetracked by all this stuff. Take this one: 'Mr. O'Hara had ten cats, each cat had four paws . . .' Well, already there's an interesting thought for you. Much more interesting than the arithmetic involved. What is Mr. O'Hara doing with ten cats? Is he a young man or a little old man who keeps cats and spends all his pension money feeding them? Are they one mama cat and nine kittens or ten strays or what? What about the strange mention of the four paws? Is this not standard issue for cats? I think they do protest too much. I think maybe one of those cats is missing a paw and I want to know how that happened. Otherwise, Doris, why do they even bother to mention it?"

"Because," said Doris patiently, "then there wouldn't be an arithmetic problem. You have to multiply the ten cats by their four paws and then figure out what would happen if three cats lost their mittens and figure how many mittens you would have in all."

"That's idiotic," I persisted. "Why don't they just say ten times four minus three?"

"Because it's not three," said Doris. "It's twelve. The three cats have four paws each and a mitten for each paw, so that's twelve mittens."

"What about the one with the missing paw? That's where they mean to trip you up."

"They're not trying to trip you up, Hortense. They're trying to prepare you for daily encounters with math. They're trying to prepare you for real life."

"Who do you know who has ten cats and goes around knitting mittens for them?" I asked Doris patiently. Real life, indeed! Doris isn't always too swift.

My sister gave a heavy sigh and stood up. "Can't you two do that someplace else? I am trying to read."

"This is *homework*!" I shouted. I shouted because I was feeling the January blues and story problems did nothing to improve my mood.

My mom came in to start supper. She had stopped throwing up and napping and was a real live wire compared to what she had been like in December.

"How's the arithmetic coming along, girls?" she asked.

"Fine, Mrs. Hemple," said Doris in her polite nicey-nice voice.

"Fine, my foot," I said. "What's for supper?"

"Stew," said my mom. "You'll have to take that homework into the den now. I want to start peeling onions on the table. How would you like a birthday party this year, Hortense?"

Wow, I thought, a birthday party. My mom has never been

very enthusiastic about me inviting friends over for a birth-day party. She let me have one in the second grade, and that's been it.

"Great," I said. "How many girls can I invite?"

"I was thinking more in terms of a family birthday party," she said.

"What do you mean?"

"It's been a long time since we've seen your aunts and uncles. We could have everyone in for dinner to celebrate your birthday."

"Oh, ugh," I said. My aunts are a real bunch of incipient biddies. Even my dad calls them the twits-in-law. I can't imag-ine what my mother was thinking.

"A family party would be so lovely," said my mother wist-fully.

I was about to say no in firm tones when Doris nudged me and said, "My relatives all came for dinner last year."

That was just like Doris, bringing her sardine-like family into it.

"Did they?" said Mom. "How nice."

"They all brought clothes for my Barbie," she finished.

I hate that old Barbie. Paper dolls are one thing, but you have to draw the line at three-dimensional dolls at our age. I'd think even Doris would see that.

"How did they know you wanted doll clothes for that old Barbie?" I asked.

"When I made out the invitations, I included a list of items I needed."

I thought including a list of things you wanted for your birthday was tacky. That was just like Doris. Sometimes she has no class. On the other hand, this was just the thing those old biddies deserved, and it would certainly save them precious shopping hours.

"Could I send out the invitations?" I asked Mom.

"Certainly," she said. "But we had better hurry and get them in the mail. Your birthday is in two weeks. Oh, and we'd better make it for the Friday night before your birthday because Daddy has basketball tickets for the next night."

"Daddy is going out on my birthday?"

"But doesn't Doris always sleep over anyway?" asked Mom, all innocence.

"I'm going to be gone for the next few weekends," said Doris. "I'm sorry I didn't tell you sooner, but my mother just told me this morning."

"I'm surprised everyone isn't leaving en masse for Paris," I snapped.

Mom sighed. "It's getting late. Why don't you take your homework into the den while I finish the stew."

When she was done, Mom drove Doris home. On the way back, she and I shopped for party invitations.

"Oh, look," she said. "These have rabbits on them."

"Let's not start that again."

I chose some invitations with clowns on the front. They had the proper festive spirit without being too babyish. The clowns were holding balloons, which I thought was a neat reminder not to arrive empty-handed. When we got home I set out writing them. There was no limit to the things I could use. There were two books of paper dolls I had my eye on. Any books by E. Nesbit would be appreciated—hard to find, it was true, but what did my aunts have to do all day, anyway? I wrote each invitation carefully, then I mailed them.

In the meantime I was having severe doubts about my

notebook project. Was it helping to organize my thoughts? I penned a note to Letitia and stuck it on her bulletin board. She might ignore me but she always answered her mail. It said:

> *Dear Fat Hips,*
> *Do you think writing everything down in a notebook can organize your life? Answer soon.*
> *Signed,*
> *Medusa*

I received an immediate reply:

> *Dear Medusa,*
> *Thank you but my life is as neat as a pin. If it is your life we are talking about, why don't you begin by shoveling out your room. Oink oink.*
> *Signed,*
> *Fat Hips*

It is just like Letitia to mock me when I am asking her for a little sisterly advice. Nonetheless, I decided to abandon my notebook. I might still write in it from time to time, but I had to come up with something more substantial to impress Aunt Kate. I finally decided that if she was going to write about the cuisine of Lower Michigan, I would take over the murder mystery writing. I spent all of the following week working on one. I had it all lined up, the suspects and the corpse. I just couldn't decide who had done it or why. I decided that it was going to take too long to write. Instead, I would just announce the intention of writing it. I knocked on Aunt Kate's door. She was typing.

"Go away," she called.

"Guess what, Aunt Kate," I yelled through the door. She didn't answer.

"I am writing a murder mystery," I called.

"Hortense, I am *working!*" she yelled.

"Well, when can we discuss this?" I asked.

"What's to discuss?" she said. "You don't discuss writing a book, you just go ahead and write it."

"Well, how about stopping off at my writing studio"— which is what I had renamed my bedroom—"before Barbara and Elise pick you up?"

"Barbara and Elise aren't picking me up tonight," she said.

"Aren't you going out with them?"

"No."

"Aren't you going out?" I asked.

"Yes, I am going out. No, I am not going out with Barbara and Elise. Yes, I am *trying* to write. Go away. This time I really mean it, Hortense."

I decided that the murder mystery idea wasn't very good. I had never read a murder mystery anyway, only seen one on TV. Also, if Aunt Kate wasn't going to discuss it with me, then there was no point at all. I would have to find a new project. I wondered who Aunt Kate was going out with. I had known her occasionally to see other people, but Saturday nights had always been spent with Cronies One and Two. Who was the mysterious stranger that she was seeing tonight? I sat by my bedroom window to see if someone would pick her up, but Aunt Kate took her own car, so I assumed she was meeting this person somewhere. Come to think of it, I thought, Cronies One and Two hadn't been over to the house at all since December, when the three of them went up north ice fishing. Hmmmm.

I could hardly wait for my birthday. I could put up with an evening with the biddies-to-be when I thought that finally I would get all the things I wanted. I had decided that this party was my due. I had put up with my family's unjustified neglect for months. I deserved some tangible compensation.

The night of my party I put on my red dress. It is a bit young for me, I fear, having ruffles all over it, but I wore it to please Mom. I wished to encourage any pathetic attempt on her part to pay a little more attention to me. She even made the kind of hors d'oeuvres I really like: bacon wrapped around water chestnuts. She serves these to her bridge club. Usually I am allowed one, but since it was my birthday she let me eat as many as I liked. There is no such thing as too much of a good thing.

I was busily chewing on a plate of them and drinking an Orange Crush. Letitia was still upstairs. Aunt Kate and Mom were being nasty and bumping into each other in the kitchen, the way they always do before a party. The main source of conflict seemed to be whether they should put the casseroles out on the buffet now before she forgot (Mom) or whether this would cause everyone to drop dead of food poisoning, besides which, the food wasn't that good to begin with (Aunt Kate). All that they could agree on was that everyone was to help herself and mill about.

My dad was trying to hide in the basement, muttering about fuses. I heard a car pull up and the first aunts arrived. It was Aunt Dee and Aunt Clara. They are unmarried and live together in Detroit. They were carrying big boxes. I racked my brain trying to think what could be in them. I hadn't asked for anything that big. Then it occurred to me that maybe they had gotten me something on my list *and* a present of their own choosing. I greeted them enthusiastically.

"Why, Aunt Dee, Aunt Clara, how nice to see you!" I called and pumped their hands. They leaned over and kissed me with their withered dry spinster lips. I kissed them back, sneaking another surreptitious look at those boxes.

"Happy birthday, Hortense dear," said Aunt Clara. "We brought your mother a little something for the baby. Could you put it over there on that bench while we take off our— Kate dear! Ada!" And they were swept into kissy-kissy with Mom and Aunt Kate.

Everyone was shrieking and more cars were pulling up. I threw the boxes on the bench. I could now see that they were tied with baby-shower-type paper. I didn't understand. Where were *my* presents? Maybe they were still in the car. Maybe Aunt Clara and Aunt Dee couldn't carry all those boxes in and were going to make another trip, only they got sidetracked by my parents.

My dad answered the door and Aunt April and Uncle Dan came in. Dad took a bassinet from them. They didn't have anything else with them. What was going on? I went over and pulled Letitia away from Aunt June and Aunt May, who had arrived without their husbands. I had to stop and kiss them, but it was perfunctory. I was feeling less enthusiastic about this whole evening.

"Listen, Letitia," I hissed, "aren't I supposed to get any presents out of this whole affair?"

"I'm not supposed to tell you," said Letitia.

"You better," I threatened.

"Oh, well, I don't care. I don't see what the big deal is anyway," she said, and grabbed a handful of peanuts. "They all got together and bought you a bond."

"A what?"

"A bond. You know, it's like stocks or something. It's money, but you can't touch it until you're grownup. Mom and Dad will probably put it toward your college education."

"Those rats. Those dirty rats," I said. I couldn't tell Letitia or anyone about putting in an order for specific presents.

Just then Aunt Kate came in.

"Get out there," she whispered. "It's rude to stay huddled like this in the kitchen, Hortense, when the party is in your honor."

"If the party is in my honor, then why is everyone bringing presents for the baby?"

"Hortense, Hortense," said Aunt Kate. "You must rise above it."

"Well, if you ask me, they're the rude ones."

"They probably won't see your mother again until after the baby is born," said Aunt Kate, grabbing a shrimp puff. "I'm sure that's the only reason they brought baby presents."

"I'm not going back out there with all those tacky people," I declared and ate two water chestnuts wrapped in bacon and a celery stick full of cream cheese.

"Ummm," said Aunt Kate. She had a mouth full of sour cream and onion soup dip. "Well, there's no reason to sink to their level, Hortense. The thing to do is go in there and be gracious and charming *anyway*."

A terrible thought occurred to me. Suppose one of the circulating aunts in the living room mentioned my demand for specific presents to my parents. It would be so humiliating. I decided I had better get out there and do a little circulating myself. Perhaps I could head them off at the pass, should the conversation swing around that way.

On my way out, my mother came swooping in. I could tell she was having a wonderful time. Her face was flushed and she was even more distracted-looking than usual.

"Having a good time, dear?" she asked me. "Kate, Clara

and April want you to sign the card for the B-O-N-D," she spelled out.

She gets loopier and loopier as the months go by.

She picked up a stack of plates. It had a Post-it on it. It read: PLATES FOR HORS D'OEUVRES. The napkins had a Post-it on them that read: BRING OUT WITH FIRST SET OF PLATES. The shrimp puffs had a Post-it that said: SERVE WHEN RUNNING LOW ON CRAB DIP. The cake plates said: FOR BIRTHDAY CAKE. I decided that until this baby was born, my mother was a dead loss.

I wandered around the room and smiled at aunts who screamed, "I can't get over how much you've grown!"

Aunt June sat me down to ask me about school.

"Ah, me," she said. "It's nice to see everyone together again. It's never much fun, dear, when you get together just for funerals."

"I can see that," I said.

"To think of Kate still living with Ada. I thought Kate would be the first of us to be snatched up."

"Snatched up?" I asked.

"Into matrimony," explained Aunt June. "She had everything, beauty, brains, common sense. She always won the awards; let's see, there was the track-and-field award, a writing award, the blue ribbon for the best apron in her home ec. class."

I giggled. This made Aunt Kate seem a little less imposing.

"I don't suppose they make aprons in home ec. anymore," said Aunt June indulgently. "Probably teach you plumbing or some other useful nonsexist skill."

"I don't know," I said. "We don't get home ec. until junior high."

"Oh, of course," said Aunt June, her eyes beginning to wander.

"Well, Aunt June," I said. "Pleasant chatting." I began to edge away.

She smiled vaguely and lit a cigarette.

"Gotta go," I mumbled and went to see if Mom had put the lasagna out yet. She had, and I filled a plate and ate moodily in the corner.

I put my dirty plate in the kitchen and wandered into the den. My dad and Uncle Dan were smoking cigars and laughing.

"Having a good time, lamb chop?" asked Dad.

"Swell," I said with enthusiasm. No sense blaming him. This wasn't his idea. These weren't even his sisters. "But I wish we could have the cake soon. I'm getting sleepy."

Dad looked at his watch. "It's only seven o'clock," he said.

"I know," I said. "But all the excitement has just worn me out." I tried to look exhausted.

"Come on, Dan," said Dad, stubbing out his cigar.

Dad got Mom. I can always count on him to rescue me from intolerable situations.

"Listen, Ada," he said. "I think Hortense is getting anxious for her cake and present. You and the girls can talk after she goes to bed."

So Mom lit the candles on the cake and everyone sang "Happy Birthday." Then they gave me the bond and applauded each other for thinking of such a neat present. I went upstairs. I suppose as soon as I dragged my weary feet up the stairs, they thought, Hurray! Let the good times roll.

After a while I got up and sat in the hall by the stairs listening to the rest of the party. I could hear Mom opening the baby presents and shrieking and everyone laughing and having a good time. Happy birthday to me.

*   *   *

On my real birthday, my father made me blueberry waffles. I decided to delete some of my nastier comments about his basketball tickets in my book of observations.

"You know," I said while moving the syrup bottle a touch closer to the birthday girl, "we ought to make a family newspaper. We could each write one column a week and Aunt Kate could type it up for us on Sunday."

"Ha!" said Letitia. "I can just see Aunt Kate taking time to type up a family newspaper."

"What column should I write?" asked my mother.

"Are you putting *more* syrup on your waffles?" asked Letitia. "You've already poured syrup twice on those same waffles."

"What column should *I* write?" asked Mom again.

"It happens to be my birthday," I said to Letitia. "You can write an animal column," I said to my mother, wondering if she would catch the reference to rabbits, heh heh heh.

"Hmmm," she said. "Animal lore. Do you wish you had a dog, Hortense? When I was a girl, my sisters and I doted on a big black Lab the neighbors kept."

"Happy diabetes to you," sang Letitia.

"Who wants another waffle?" asked Dad.

"I don't like dogs," I said.

"Some orange juice?" asked Dad.

"His name was Lucky," said Mom, staring out the window as if her old neighbors still lived next door and she would catch a glimpse of them if she looked hard enough.

"Why don't you open your presents?" said Letitia, pushing a pile of them toward me.

"Lucky Luciano," said Mom dreamily.

"They named their dog after a gangster?" asked Letitia.

"Not at first. That's what we called him after he bit the mailman."

"I've never liked dogs," I said again, ripping the paper off my presents.

Letitia gave me sealing wax and a new seal. My parents gave me some clothes, and my mom gave me a new dress for my Barbie. She hasn't noticed that I haven't played with my Barbie for a whole year, but as I've been saying, she's a dead loss anyway. I wrote HAPPY BIRTHDAY on a Post-it and stuck it on my forehead. The irony was apparently lost on Mom.

At lunch Aunt Kate gave me a new dress and Authors, which turned out to be a pretty good card game, and since it was Saturday, she played it with me all afternoon, which is most unlike her.

Doris came over right before dinner and gave me a new book of paper dolls. She was leaving for Holland, Michigan, to spend the rest of the weekend with her grandparents.

It wasn't such a bad birthday, it just didn't meet my expectations, and I felt let down. Letitia left for Kathy's, and I could hear Aunt Kate getting ready to go out. I knew she was reviewing a really nice restaurant because she had told me. I got into bed early with my new paper dolls and built them a Sears, Roebuck house among the sheets and pillows. There was a knock on the door.

"Who is it?" I asked.

"It's Aunt Kate," came her crisp voice. I jumped up. Aunt Kate never visits me in my room.

"Hello, Hortense," she said. She really looked beautiful. She was wearing a pale green silk dress with gold jewelry and she smelled good.

"I hope you like the dress I gave you," she said, "but if you don't, I will take you shopping to exchange it."

"It's nice," I said. It was, too. Aunt Kate's got good taste, that's for sure.

"I wanted to take you out for dinner tonight and give you a chance to break it in, but I have to review a restaurant. Perhaps, in honor of your birthday, you would like to go out with me next Saturday night."

Could I believe my ears? Even Letitia had never been out alone with Aunt Kate.

"Oh, that would be great!" I cried.

"Well, fine," said Aunt Kate and took her date book out of her purse. I had seen her write things in it before, but here she was putting *our* date in it. That really made me feel grownup and sophisticated.

"Let's see," she said, flipping pages, "that will be February the second. Let's say sixish."

"Sixish it is," I said, trying to sound suave and cool.

"Happy birthday, then, Hortense," she said, exiting.

I followed her to the door.

"Have a good time," I called after her and then hopped in my bed, but I was too excited to continue with my paper dolls. Perhaps my relentless pursuit of worthy projects was beginning to break down her natural reserve. She hadn't seemed too impressed with either my notebook or my murder mystery idea, but maybe *subconsciously* she was impressed! I got out my green Walgreen's notebook and scribbled out every nasty thing I had written about Aunt Kate.

February

~~~~~~

I thought the week waiting for my date with Aunt Kate would never end. I spent a lot of time during arithmetic wondering where we would go. I hoped Aunt Kate wouldn't ask me about my big absorbing project because not one had panned out so far. Of course, originally I had planned to write a lot in my book of secret observations, then in January I had decided to abandon it when I found it was not helping me organize my life. I had since picked it up from time to time but found I only used it to make nasty remarks about people I was mad at. I had even tired of keeping track of my mother's lunacies. Nevertheless, it had worked out better than the color-coded sock idea, which went nowhere. I still used the notebook to write an occasional bit about Virginia Vermeulen because I was nervous about her. She watched me at school.

On Monday she was passing by my desk and she started

to hum the "Bunny Hop" under her breath. I sat tense and poised, but that was all she did.

"That old Virginia Vermeulen," I said to Doris during lunch. She was eating a hard-boiled egg.

Doris always has the same lunch, and she always eats it the same way. First there is her hard-boiled egg, which she slowly unwraps and eats in tiny bites. Next she has her four cheese slices with her corresponding four crackers. Then her apple slices. Her thermos of soup follows, to be eaten with her little soup spoon. Finally, she always gets one of her mother's homemade cookies, and when it is molasses, I try not to think about it.

"What's she done now?" asked Doris.

"You know this stupid rabbit game my mom and dad play?"

Doris nodded.

"Well, my mom was hopping around the Vermeulens' orchard in October, and Virginia saw her and now she won't let me forget it. Every so often she does something sly like sing the 'Bunny Hop,' or she tries to catch my eye when we pass each other in the hall, and I'm sure she is going to say something about it."

"As long as she doesn't fink on you publicly," said Doris. Doris has a great fear of being publicly finked on. Usually I find this cowardly, but this time I could see eye to eye with her.

"Speak of the devil," said Doris in a low voice because there was Virginia approaching our lunch table.

She was wearing low-slung jeans and a black T-shirt with a yellow cardigan over it. The cardigan had a hole in one sleeve. She had on high-top black sneakers. Around her neck hung blue beads. It was tacky.

"Hi, guys," she said and snapped her gum.

I tried to look tough. Doris looked extra-prim.

"So, how's tricks?" asked Virginia, leaning forward and putting her hands on the lunch table.

"First of all," said Doris, "we're not guys."

"Oh, excuse me," said Virginia. "Hey, you." She turned to me.

I had the feeling I was about to be finked on in public.

"How's your ma?"

"Fine," I mumbled. I was afraid at this point of provoking her.

"I hear she's got a bun in the oven."

Vulgar.

"Yeah," I said.

"How about that."

"If it's any of *your* business," said Doris, beginning to stuff her half-eaten lunch into her bag. This took a little while because she had to carefully rewrap everything in cellophane. It mesmerized Virginia. Doris, I have noticed, while usually too, too polite, can be perfectly awful to people she considers beneath her. I could see that Doris was bent on escape. All in all, it seemed like a good move. I shoved the rest of my bologna sandwich back in the bag with the open bag of Fritos.

Doris stood up and grabbed the corner of my sleeve, pulling me to my feet. "Goodbye," she said coldly to Virginia.

"Mine too," said Virginia and sat down where Doris had been sitting. Doris and I walked all the way to the front doors of the school and sat on the ledge by the big windows to finish our lunches.

"Narrow escape." She pulled out her hard-boiled egg

again. "I thought for sure she was going to say something in that loud, awful voice."

"I thought so, too," I said, nibbling my Fritos, but something was bothering me. I calmed down and took a deep breath.

"What do you think she meant by 'mine too'?"

Doris put a cheese slice meticulously upon a cracker and contemplated it. "Who cares?" she said finally. "Do you know Virginia thinks she's too cool to bring lunch? She buys a hot dog across the street every day. I don't know what my mother would say if I bought a hot dog every day. That hot-dog stand is filthy."

If someone gave me money, I would go across the street for hot dogs, too, but I didn't dare tell Doris this.

"Well," I said, "at least I wasn't finked on in public. Do you want to come to my house after school?"

"I can't," said Doris, brushing the crumbs off her skirt. She has to brush every least crumb off or she itches all day. "I have a ballet lesson."

"Give me a break," I said. "You don't take ballet."

"I do now. I just started. I plan to become a ballerina when I grow up."

"Oh, brother," I said. It was the only thing I could think of to say. For some reason I didn't want Doris to take ballet lessons. Not without me. Not that I wanted to become a ballerina. I certainly did not.

"Maybe I will try to join, too," I said.

"You can't," said Doris as we started to head back to class together. "You have to be a certain type. You have to have long legs."

I wouldn't have minded if she had said this in a matter-of-fact way. I would be the first to admit that Doris looks the part with her long, thin everything. The more I thought about it, the more I thought that she resembled a snake with blond hair. I might have said a swan had she been matter-of-fact and not so smug. I also admit that I am more the gopher sort myself, with just ordinary stubby legs and brown, fuzzy hair. Doris clearly didn't want me to take ballet with her. I didn't talk to her the rest of the week.

By Saturday I was ready to make up with her so that I could tell her Sunday morning how my date with Aunt Kate had gone. Then I remembered she had left for Traverse City to visit her cousins. Her family could save a lot of money by just deciding on one city and all moving there.

I was in quite a dither all day Saturday. I heard the buzz and bang of Aunt Kate's typewriter in the afternoon. At four o'clock I took a bath because I wanted to be clean and good-smelling. I took some of Letitia's bubble bath and put it in the tub. It was called Gardenia Evening and it really smelled awful, but I didn't want to smell like plain old soap if Aunt Kate was taking me somewhere sophisticated. At five o'clock I put on my new dress, and at six o'clock Aunt Kate knocked on my door.

"Are you ready?" she asked.

I came out. She was wearing a skirt, a sweater, and a blazer. She looked very nice but not as nice as she did in her silk dress, so I figured while we weren't going to toss down a burger at McDonald's, we weren't going to the Ritz either. That was okay by me. Really fancy restaurants make me too nervous to enjoy my food.

We got into Aunt Kate's little red car. It has bucket seats, and when I sit in it I feel like I am disappearing below the dash, never to be seen again. Tonight I didn't mind because

I was a tad shy. I had the uncomfortable feeling you get when someone is being extra nice to you.

"Where are we going for dinner? Knapper's?" I asked finally.

Aunt Kate came out of her semiperpetual fog. "No, indeed," she said. "We are going to an Indian restaurant."

"Oh." I tried not to sound disappointed, but I had been salivating for some nice fried chicken. "Can I get chicken at an Indian restaurant?"

"Certainly. You can get tandoori chicken, which is chicken baked in a special clay oven. The chicken becomes buttery-tender."

"Have you ever reviewed this restaurant?" I asked.

"Once, a couple of years ago," said Aunt Kate. "It's quite a nice restaurant. I wanted to take you someplace different."

The wind was blowing freezing pellets. We had to park three blocks from the Star of India, so the first blast of warm air as we entered was doubly welcome. The walls were all gold and red. It was candle-lit and dim and smelled exotically spicy. It was the type of place where someone should be murdered. I tried to look inscrutable as the waiter led us to our table.

"What's that strange expression on your face?" hissed Aunt Kate.

"Do you think this restaurant is a front?" I asked.

"A what?" asked Aunt Kate.

"A front." The waiter brought our menus, so we didn't say anything until he disappeared again.

"A front for what?"

"Who knows?" I asked darkly.

Aunt Kate snorted.

"Doesn't it make you feel inscrutable?"

"No," said Aunt Kate. "I find it cozy. There's something atavistic about restaurants in winter."

"At a what?" I asked.

"Atavistic. We remember coming out of the cold to a dark cave, a warm fire, and a bowl of dinosaur soup."

The food was spicy. I was very proud of myself for eating even the mysterious red and orange vegetable-looking things. I began to feel pretty exotic myself. Soon I realized we were dressed all wrong. I imagined us in flapper-type clothes, sailing on a luxury liner. Do not ask me why I lapsed into this fantasy. It must have been something in the curry.

"You know," I said to Aunt Kate, "I've been thinking about this food book you're writing."

"Mmm," she said, because her mouth was full.

"Wouldn't it be fun to write it together? I mean, that way we could have two points of view. Don't be too hasty in your response," I added, because she was about to say something. "I'd describe tonight's dinner as spicy and interesting. The chicken was good and the sauces were very good, say seven on a one-to-ten scale. I'd recommend this restaurant, wouldn't you?"

"What happened to your murder mystery?" asked Aunt Kate.

"*Finito*," I said.

"That laundry thing you mentioned?"

"A passing fancy."

"I don't think I could depend on you, Hortense. Besides which, you don't know anything about food or restaurants or writing and you are only ten years old."

Trust Aunt Kate not to mince her words.

"And now," said Aunt Kate as we leaned back in our chairs

and she sipped some tea, "what shall we do with the rest of our evening?"

I was full and warm, and I could have curled up in a ball under the table and gone to sleep quite happily, but that wouldn't have been sporting.

"What would *you* like to do?" I asked Aunt Kate politely.

When I ask Doris this, she then asks me what I would like to do and then I ask her what she would like to do and then she asks me what I would like to do, so eventually it gets back to me and I get my way while seeming to be polite. But Aunt Kate obviously isn't familiar with this social convention.

"I think I would like to go hear some music," said Aunt Kate.

I sighed, since I knew I wouldn't be allowed in a bar. This meant the evening was over as far as I was concerned.

"Would you like to come too?" asked Aunt Kate.

"You bet," I said.

We bundled into our coats and drove off into the night. The lights were glaringly bright. It was eight-thirty, and the evening was just beginning. No wonder Aunt Kate didn't get up until noon. We drove a long way, right out past the outskirts of Riverside, until we came to a big old barn.

"This is the Bakerfield restaurant," said Aunt Kate. "I know someone who is playing here tonight. I thought we'd have dessert and listen for an hour."

We were ushered to a table. Boy, was I surprised to see who was playing guitar and singing songs. It was Old Crazy Joe. We call him that because he lives in an abandoned caboose in the woods. All the kids know about him. You see him walking around downtown sometimes. He's got kind of shaggy hair and a beard. He is long, tall, and ragged like a scarecrow. I give him a wide berth. I never knew he *did* anything. I certainly didn't know he could sing.

Aunt Kate ordered crepes Suzettes for us. I'd never eaten anything flaming before. It turns out you don't eat the flames. Crepes Suzettes are just pancakes, really. I would have preferred a hot fudge sundae, but you don't tell Aunt Kate things like that. Aunt Kate thinks everyone should speak their mind as long as it agrees with what she thinks.

"I didn't know you knew Old Crazy Joe," I said, scraping my plate.

"Who?" asked Aunt Kate.

"Old Crazy Joe. You know, that guy up there singing."

"In the first place, Hortense," said Aunt Kate, "his name is Joseph Baker, *Mr.* Baker to you, and he is a musician. He is *not* old, nor is he crazy. Do you understand?"

"He lives in a caboose, Aunt Kate," I said, defending my position.

"So what? The caboose has been fixed up and insulated, and it's really nicer than a lot of homes I've been in."

"You've been in Old—er—Mr. Baker's caboose?" I asked incredulously.

"Certainly," said Aunt Kate. "Sssh, he's coming over."

I wished I had some more crepes Suzettes left so I had something to fidget with. I grabbed a packet of crackers from the basket on the table and crumbled them. I don't think you are supposed to eat the crackers if you've only ordered dessert, but this was an emergency.

"Hullo, Kate," said Old Crazy Joe, pulling out a chair and swinging one long stringy leg over it.

"Hullo, Joe," said Aunt Kate, smiling at him in an especially nice way. "This is my niece, Hortense."

"Hullo, Hortense," said Old Crazy Joe, holding out a hand for me to shake. I had to shake it, but it gave me the creeps.

"Happy birthday," he said.

So she had told him it was my birthday, too. Apparently they were real chums. I had an inkling of what had happened to Cronies One and Two. If Aunt Kate had stopped seeing them because she wanted to see more of Old Joe, she must be serious about him. And since this was the first romantic liaison I had known her to have, I was pretty excited. Especially since I have always suspected that she was cruelly jilted in her salad days. In books, anyhow, this is generally why the heroine remains unwed. I wondered if Aunt Kate had brought me here for the express purpose of meeting Joe. On the other hand, it was more likely that I was the last thing on her mind when she decided to come here. Was she going to be so wrapped up with him that there was no chance for me to develop an intimate relationship with her? She sure seemed impressed with *him* all right, and I wondered what he had that I didn't. There wasn't even a *hint* of disparagement in her voice when she spoke to him.

"You sounded good tonight, Joe," said Aunt Kate.

"Thanks." He nodded. "Can I order you something? Coffee? Coke for you, Hortense?" He looked right at me. He had piercing eyes, and I wanted to slide under the table and hide. He didn't seem crazy. In fact, he seemed nice, but I wasn't used to being treated like a grownup all evening, and it was beginning to wear on me—especially after all that food.

Luckily, Aunt Kate answered for us. "We just stopped for dessert, and now I really think we must be going."

"See you up north next weekend, then?" asked Old Crazy Joe.

"Right," said Aunt Kate. "I'll talk to you before then, anyway."

We stood up to leave.

"Is that why you go up north? To meet Mr. Baker?" I asked her excitedly after we had climbed into the car.

"He goes fishing by Petoskey, which is, coincidentally, where I go fishing. I met him when I was on a fishing trip with Barbara and Elise," said Aunt Kate in an end-the-discussion voice.

"I didn't know you went up by Petoskey," I said.

"There's a lot you don't know," said Aunt Kate.

I dropped the subject. I didn't want to ruin the evening.

"Well, thanks," I said when we pulled up at the door.

"You're welcome," said Aunt Kate, not turning the motor off. "You go on; I'm going out for a while."

I ran into the house. Mom was sitting at the kitchen table eating cornflakes and reading the back of the box. Dad was in the den watching TV and smoking a cigar.

"Did you have a good time, darling?" asked Mom with her mouth full.

"Oh, yes," I said, plopping down opposite her. I watched her in disgusted fascination. When she had finished the cornflakes, she got out the chocolate chip cookies that I had made that Wednesday and smeared one with cream cheese.

"Where did you go?" she asked with her mouth full again. Honestly, it was like she couldn't take time out from chowing down to have a decent conversation.

"To an Indian restaurant and then to Bakerfield restaurant for crepes Suzettes," I said.

"Where's Aunt Kate?"

"She went out again," I said.

"Oh, well," said Mom, digging around now on the bottom

shelf of the fridge. I noticed that she was getting kind of fat. Not just her stomach either, but all over. Our grocery bills must be enormous. She opened a jar of herring and began eating out of it.

"Hey," I protested. "You always tell me never to eat out of the jar."

"I'm going to finish what's in the jar," she said with a piece of onion hanging out of her mouth. This was unbelievable. "It's okay to eat out of the jar if you plan to finish it."

"Where's Letitia?" I asked.

"She's sleeping at Kathy's," said Mom.

"Again?" I asked because she had slept there the last three Saturdays in a row. If she slept there much more, Kathy's family might as well adopt her.

"Well, they're very tight these days. I wrote an animal lore column for our family newspaper, Hortense. Do you want to see it?"

"Oooh, ever so sorry," said my evil twin. "I have changed your column to 'Happy Reminiscences about Our Family, Particularly of Hortense.' "

"Hmmm," said Mom, seriously contemplating this. "Are you going to church with us tomorrow?"

"What do you mean? I *always* go to church with you."

"You'd better get to bed, then. It's getting late."

I gave her a hug. She managed to put the herring down long enough to hug me back.

I got into bed and just sat there. I was sleepy, but there was so much to think about I couldn't fall asleep. Aunt Kate and Old Crazy Joe. I couldn't believe it. If Aunt Kate was going to date anyone, I would think it would be someone terribly sophisticated like a symphony conductor or something. I mean, if gentlemen who lived in cabooses could get her attention, how come I was having such a hard time? Mind you, she had taken me out to dinner. That was a good sign even if her manner toward me hadn't noticeably warmed up.

Why didn't Doris want me in her ballet class?

What had Virginia Vermeulen meant by "mine too"? At first when she said that, I thought she meant her mother was going to have a baby, but the Vermeulens already had seven kids in their family. Still, I suppose that didn't mean there couldn't be an eighth. Mrs. Vermeulen looked so old. Even older than my mom. I lay there and tossed and turned, and finally I got out my stationery and wrote to Letitia.

> *Dear Fat Hips,*
> *I think Mrs. Vermeulen is having another baby.*
> *Sincerely,*
> *Medusa*

I stuck the note on her bulletin board and lay down again.

I wanted to write to Letitia about Aunt Kate and Old Crazy Joe, but I figured she'd probably just say "So what?" because that's what she always says these days. I would like to tell Doris, but Doris is so prim. She would be mortified that she knew someone who had an aunt who was dating Old Crazy Joe. I wouldn't tell Mom anything important these days. It is a very lonely thing to have no one to tell your pressing secrets to. I felt cold and lonely the rest of February.

March

~~~~~~

When March came, there was still snow on the ground, which I didn't mind because I knew it could warm up and disappear within a week. I put on my new tennis shoes and stuffed my winter boots in the back of the closet. One of the first signs of spring is when you stop moving along like a train (chug, chug, chug) and start to bounce.

The second Tuesday in March, I felt especially springy even though it was cold out. Dinner wouldn't be ready until six and my homework was done. Letitia was in her room with Kathy. Aunt Kate was up north for the week. It seemed she had abandoned her book about the cuisine of Lower Michigan in favor of the cuisine of Upper Michigan. I decided to trot down to Mrs. Beddoe's house. Mrs. Beddoe is Doris's ballet teacher. Doris takes ballet class in Mrs. Beddoe's basement from four until five on Tuesdays.

At five o'clock, out came Doris looking soulful. I guess all that ballet for a whole hour really gets to you in the end.

"Hi," I said, acting a little too perfectly normal to cover up my embarrassment. I wasn't sure how she'd react to my sudden appearance. "I figured I could walk you home."

"Hi," said Doris, also acting too perfectly normal. She was carrying a vinyl case with a picture of a ballerina on the front. I wouldn't have been caught dead with it, myself.

"Can you sleep over Saturday night?" I asked as we walked along.

"I'm sleeping over at Debbie Springfield's," she said.

Debbie Springfield's mom teaches the third grade at our school. Debbie has one of those perky personalities so popular with all types of people. Everyone wants to sleep over at Debbie's house because her mom buys you a toy when you sleep there. Nothing big, but a jump rope or something. I have never had the pleasure myself, but I have heard this from three reliable sorts during the usual recess gossip. Also, if you sleep over, there's a chance you will get invited to go to lunch with Debbie and her mom. Once a month Debbie's mom takes Debbie and a friend to Howard Johnson's. Our family used to go out to dinner every payday—McDonald's or something. In our family, Howard Johnson's is only for birthdays. These days we have dinner at home on payday. It is just another warning sign, if you ask me.

"Maybe you will get to go to lunch at Howard Johnson's, you lucky duck," I said to her.

"I am. Next Saturday," said Doris a bit smugly.

I'd rather go to Howard Johnson's than some old Indian restaurant anyday.

We had reached Doris's house. I thought she would at least ask me in for a cookie. Doris's house is a long way

from our house, and it had been particularly considerate of
me to pick her up and walk her home.

"My mom probably has dinner ready, and I have to take
a bath after my ballet class," said Doris, standing at the door
and not letting me in.

"Oh, really." I sniffed. I turned around and stalked off.
There is only so much abuse I will take from Doris. I don't
like her to forget that I am the more desirable friend. When
I first met Doris, she was a little pool of wimpdom and
nobody wanted to have anything to do with her. Lucky for
her I came along. So what did Debbie see in her all of a
sudden? It was extremely annoying. I could tell that Doris
was all puffed up over her ballet classes and now this lunch
invitation. I slushed home and came in late for dinner.

It didn't matter because it turned out Mom had left a meat
loaf in the oven, which my dad and Letitia were just getting
out.

"Mom is going to be late. She went to the wholesaler's
with Mrs. Wilson," explained Dad.

Mrs. Wilson is our neighbor who runs a health food store.

"What did she want to go to the wholesaler's for?" I asked.

"Mrs. Wilson has to make a buy, and she said that if Mom
saw anything she wanted, she would pick it up for her whole-
sale."

"Like what?" asked Letitia. "All Mrs. Wilson sells is that
awful health food stuff that goes moldy in three days."

"They have all kinds of stuff at the wholesaler's," said Dad.

We sat around the table and ate the meat loaf.

"How's school?" asked Dad.

That is just about the dreariest question in the world, but
you have to give my dad credit for trying. Letitia brushed it
aside.

"Dad," she asked, "what are you going to name the baby?"

"Well, we haven't decided for sure, but we were thinking of Maxine."

"Maxine?" I screeched. "That's horrible."

"I'll say," agreed Letitia. "That's as bad as Letitia and Hortense. You might at least try to give one of us a *normal* name. How about Ashley?"

"Everyone is named Ashley these days," said Dad. "I think Maxine is very nice."

"It is not," insisted Letitia. "It sounds like some big dumb blonde who pops her gum."

"Well . . ." said Dad. My dad is too easily swayed by Letitia. He tries to be judicious, but one can be too judicious with Letitia. You have to fight tooth and nail with her. As much as I disliked the name Maxine, I disliked seeing Dad bullied even more.

Just then Mom came staggering in under a huge carton. Dad leaped up to get it. Mom collapsed in a chair, reached over, and took a bite of my meat loaf.

"Hey!" I said. Where were her manners?

"Guess what I bought?" she said, still panting a little.

"Cornflakes," said Dad, reading the carton.

"What a steal. You get them for *nothing* when you buy them this way."

"Well, we can always use them," said Dad a bit uncertainly.

"Oh, my God," said Letitia. "You're never going to eat all those cornflakes. How many boxes in that carton?"

"Six dozen," said Mom.

"Six dozen in that carton?" asked Letitia.

"I got six dozen in all. That counts the two cartons in the garage. I figured we could start on this."

"Even *you* can't eat that many cornflakes," said Letitia.

"Not without help," said Mom, fixing herself a plate. I was glad, because if she grabbed my meat loaf again, I was going to have to slap her little wrist. "There're recipes on the sides of the box. Tomorrow night I am going to make cornflake chicken and cornflake soufflé."

"Tomorrow night I am going to eat at Kathy's," said Letitia.

You wouldn't believe the number of things you can do with cornflakes: cornflake chicken, cornflake pudding, cornflake cookies, cornflake hamburgers, cornflake surprise. We became involuntary experts. On Friday night Dad offered to take us all out for dinner, and it wasn't even payday. We leaped at the opportunity, even Letitia, who normally doesn't like to be seen in public with us.

"Where shall we go?" he asked us as we bundled into the car.

My sister wanted to go to the Indian restaurant where Aunt Kate had taken me. Mom wanted to go to McDonald's. She is very money-conscious these days and couldn't understand why we wouldn't stay home and eat more cornflakes. I said I wanted to go to Howard Johnson's. To my surprise, Dad agreed.

The parking lot was full, it being a Friday night and Howard Johnson's being a hopping place on the weekend. We waited for a table at the place where you are supposed to wait. I am always embarrassed standing there because I feel like the whole restaurant is watching me. I was idly gazing around the room when I spotted Debbie and her mom and dad and Doris all eating together. I couldn't believe it. Doris was becoming a fixture in their family. Was she going to eat at Howard Johnson's Friday night *and* Saturday lunch?

Didn't these people ever eat at home? Doris was certainly going to waddle around the dance studio next week, but this was small comfort.

"Hortense"—my mother nudged me—"isn't that Doris over there with the Springfields?"

"Oh," I said, pretending to see her for the first time. "So it is."

"Why don't you run over and say hello, darling?" asked Mom.

"I wouldn't want to disturb them," I mumbled and tried to sidle around my mom out of view of Doris.

"Didn't you say Doris was sleeping over at Debbie's tomorrow night?" asked Mom innocently.

"Yeah," I said.

"Why don't you invite both of them over some night?" she asked.

"Because Debbie and I are *not* friends," I barked. Sometimes my mom is so obtuse. "If Doris wants to have other friends, it doesn't mean I have to invite them over. Why don't you just mind your own business?"

"HORTENSE HEMPLE!" bellowed my mother in a voice so loud that several tables, including the Springfields', looked our way. Doris saw me, but she deliberately turned away.

I couldn't enjoy the fried clams that followed. My dad let us order anything for dessert, and you know what that is like at Howard Johnson's. Even Letitia abandoned her diet for a big sundae, but I was too mad at everyone to enjoy it. When we got outside, it had started to snow. Usually when it snows in March, it sends me into the depths of despair, but alas, I was already there. On the way home I curled up in the back seat and feigned sleep, but I was thinking hard. I decided enough was enough. There was only so far I could go to humor my mother and her childbearing whims. I was going to get rid of those cornflakes. She had plenty of ideas for them and so did I. I could drop two boxes off at the food depot tomorrow. Riverside has a continuous food drive. Packaged goods are distributed to the poor. If I got rid of the boxes in a slow but steady stream, she would never suspect anything.

The next morning it was very quiet, the way it is after a big snow. I looked out the window, and we had had a bunch dumped on us all right. I went downstairs and ate a piece of toast and watched Dad shovel out the drive. I didn't have anyone to play with. I sure wasn't going to call Doris.

I went into the nursery. My mother was painting it pale yellow. There was a wallpaper border of daisies around the middle of the wall. My mom had even made pale yellow curtains to match the walls. My room is white with plain blue curtains. There are fingerprints on my walls, especially around the light switch.

"I think it is time we painted my room," I announced.

Mom, who was on all fours painting the lower part of the wall, sat back on her heels and teetered there. Her stomach stuck out in front of her.

"You're going to get paint on the baby," I said coldly. I wanted to say something nastier, but these days I felt sometimes like I was standing on the shore of a desert island surrounded by members of my family, each on their own raft, gently bobbing about on the outgoing tide. I was afraid to make waves that would carry them away any faster.

"I've got my column ready for the newspaper," Mom said. "Would you like to read it?"

I was a bit embarrassed because, to be honest, I had forgotten all about the family newspaper. It had seemed like a good idea, but I hadn't really had time to get it organized. I wasn't sure when I would have the time. On the other hand, I did not wish to discourage my mother from taking part in family projects.

"Happy reminiscences about Hortense?" I asked.

"Yes, and Letitia, too. You remember the time the two of you ran around the garage in different directions and banged right into each other? You both had black eyes for a month. I called you my little family of raccoons."

That was her idea of a happy memory? "It's a good start," I said as tactfully as I could. "I'll hang on to it and edit it and let you know."

"Let me know what?" asked my mom.

"Whether we can use it."

"Is Letitia doing this with you?"

"I was using the editorial 'we,' " I said coldly. "So, when are you going to paint my room?"

"I don't know if I'll have time to paint your room," she said. "I have an awful lot to do to get this nursery ready."

"Looks ready to me," I said.

"It's too bad we gave away all the baby things," sighed Mom. "But we honestly didn't think this day would ever come. What color would you like your room?"

"Purple," I said. This was something I had been thinking about for some time.

"Well, I'll tell you what," said Mom, "if I can get the nursery finished before I grow too enormous, I will paint your room. But not purple. That's too dark. How about lavender?"

I thought about it. "How about lavender with purple curtains?"

"Okay. If I have time. No promises."

"How about having a happy family party tonight?" I asked.

We used to have happy family parties every Saturday night. We would pick up a pizza, buy some Hawaiian Punch for Letitia and me and some Tab for my mom, and Mom would pop corn. Then, after my parents had watched Lawrence Welk reruns, which they sit and snicker at because they think it's so dumb (except I think Dad secretly likes it—sometimes during the dance sequences he gets this engrossed look on his face), we would settle down and watch the circus. I don't really like the circus all that much, but I like happy family parties.

"Gee," said Mom. "A happy family party. I had almost forgotten about those, it's been so long. Well, if you can convince Letitia to stay home tonight, that would be dandy. I'll go to the grocery store this afternoon and get some Hawaiian Punch and Jiffy Pop."

"Maybe I'll even invite Aunt Kate," I said.

"You know Aunt Kate never comes to our happy family parties, but go ahead and ask if you want."

I went up to Aunt Kate's room. I hadn't thought of any new projects except the newspaper, and we all know how well that was going, but I thought maybe my new angle could be that I had no project and needed Aunt Kate's expert advice about one.

"Aunt Kate?" I called through the door.

She opened it. She had on a cold cream mask with green stuff under her eyes. I jumped.

"What are you doing?" I asked.

"I am giving myself a facial."

"Oh," I said. "I thought maybe you'd like to come to our happy family party tonight."

"That's the pizza, popcorn affair, is it?" she asked, swishing back into her room with me at her heels.

"That's right." I wondered how she knew this, since she was usually gone before it began.

"Delectable as it sounds, I have a date at Chez Louie's," she said.

Chez Louie's is Riverside's most expensive restaurant. It is Tex-French, whatever that is. I know because they have big ads in the paper saying they are Michigan's only Tex-French restaurant. "Are you reviewing it?" I asked.

"No, I am not," said Aunt Kate, smearing more green stuff under her eyes.

"Are you going with Mr. Baker?" I asked.

"Yes, I am. What is this, the Inquisition?"

"You know, I have *definitely* decided not to write a murder mystery," I said. I had already told her this, but I figured she might have forgotten.

"Well, I'm sure that's a great relief to Agatha Christie."

"Isn't she dead?"

"Very good. I didn't think you'd know who she was."

"I'm not a total ignoramus, Aunt Kate."

"What do you want, Hortense?"

"I can't think of another project," I said glumly.

"I don't know why you are so obsessed with this business of a project," she said.

"It was *your* idea," I said.

"Was it?" she said without apparent interest. "Well, it couldn't have been one of my better ones. I have to take this stuff off my face now, so . . ." she said, walking over and standing by the open door.

"See you. If you think of any ideas for a good project, feel free to visit me in my room," I said.

"I'll keep that in mind," she said, shutting the door.

I went down the hall to Letitia's room. I didn't bother to knock but barged right in.

She was sitting on her bed with cotton balls stuck between her toes, painting her toenails yellow and black. Her feet looked like they had ten bumblebees stuck to the ends of them. She had her ear to the phone.

"Just a second, my repulsive little sister just came in," she said.

"We are having a happy family party tonight," I announced coldly.

"I'm busy," said Letitia equally coldly.

"This is the first happy family party we have had since I can't remember and you *would* be busy," I said fiercely.

"Well," said Letitia, looking startled, "what kind of pizza are we going to have?"

Letitia likes pizza with sausage and I like it with pepperoni.

"Sausage," I said. "And Hawaiian Punch and Jiffy Pop."

"I no longer drink that sugary stuff," she said. "Go away and I will finish my arrangements with Kathy and then I will let you know whether I can squeeze you in before I go out tonight."

I went back to my room seething and wondered if it was worth it. She came in shortly afterward.

"You will be delighted to hear that you can count me in. Sausage pizza and no butter on the popcorn."

"All right," I conceded. I went to the nursery to find Mom and tell her she could make the food arrangements.

"Are you really going to name the baby Maxine?" I asked, settling down in the middle of the floor.

"That's one of the names we thought about," she said. "If you were going to name your sister, what would you call her?"

"Elizabeth," I said. "Elizabeth has a lot of dignity and you have a lot of choices for nicknames. Like Liz or Beth or Eliza or Betty."

"Or Zabeth or Iza," said Mom.

I wished for once she would be serious.

"Don't you think Elizabeth is a little square, Hortense? Wouldn't you rather she had a distinctive name? I like Evangeline."

"Oh, yuk," I said.

"Or Geraldina."

"Puke."

"And you know your father has a fondness for Maxine. Max for short."

"That's just horrible," I pointed out.

"How about," said my mother, beginning to look dreamy-eyed and painting rhythmically, "Rowena Matilda." She painted in time to the syllables. "Rowena." Swish, swish, swish. "Matilda." Swish, swish, swish. "Rowena Matilda. Rowena Matilda. Rowena Matilda." Swish, swish, swish. Swish, swish, swish.

As I tiptoed quietly out, I wondered if she was quite sane. I put my boots on. The snow was too deep for tennis shoes, and I had to return my books to the library. The Edward Eagers had been wonderful, but the three new books had been so bad that I don't think they had progressed my brain one bit. I grabbed my books and put them in a shopping bag with two boxes of cornflakes that I was going to drop off at the food depot. At the library I got out two E. Nesbits and three new books. By the time I got home it was almost happy family time.

The pizza was in the oven and my parents were watching Lawrence Welk. The Tab and Hawaiian Punch were on ice. I called Letitia and she came downstairs and cut herself a piece of pizza.

"Hey, you're not supposed to eat that until the circus comes on," I said.

"Do you have to turn this into a ritual?" she said with cheese running down her chin.

My dad came in from the den. "Almost circus time," he said.

Mom came in and popped the corn and put pizza pieces on paper plates for everyone. We all grabbed a drink and sat down, Mom in the big armchair, Dad in the wooden chair with the footstool, and Letitia and I on the floor at their feet. It was close, crowded, and happy. The circus came on and they were into the grand parade when the phone rang. Letitia leaped up to get it, since it is usually for her. When she returned, she was wearing her coat.

"Hey," I said. "It's happy family time."

"Can't. Plans have changed. Kathy and I just got invited to a party. Her dad's going to bring us home around eleven o'clock. Okay, Mom?"

"All right, dear, but no later than that," said Mom.

"What do you mean 'all right'?" I snapped. "This was supposed to be happy family time."

"Happy family time is not a forced march," said Letitia.

"Maybe we'll try again next week," said Mom.

"Oh, right. Sure," I said, stomping into the kitchen.

"Hortense, come on back," said Dad. "Don't you want to watch the circus?"

"I hate the circus," I said and sat down at the kitchen table to sulk in peace.

My mother came into the kitchen. "Oh, well," she said to me. I guess that was the extent of her maternal wisdom. She opened a can of anchovies and carried it back to the den. I followed her dejectedly. They had turned on Lawrence Welk again.

"I feel so restless this evening," Mom said. She was heaping extra anchovies on her piece of pizza.

"Watch the salt," said Dad.

"Mind your own business," she said, emptying the can and licking her fingers. "All this snow makes me feel under siege."

"Umm," said Dad. He wasn't paying any attention to her, I could tell. Probably he was fed up with her eating habits.

"I feel like going sledding," she said, looking pensively out the window. "Hortense, where are all our sleds?"

We have a big hill behind our house, and she was eyeing it speculatively.

"Letitia gave hers to Goodwill and mine is over at Doris's," I said. I keep it at Doris's house because she and I usually go sledding over there. That reminded me that if things kept up this way with Doris, I had better get my sled back.

"Why don't you just run over and get it, dear?" she asked.

"It's *dark* out," I reminded her. Honestly. What kind of a mother had she become?

"Daddy could drive you over."

"Their family decided suddenly to go to Holland for the weekend," I said. I was lying. Actually, this was one of the rare weekends they were spending in town, but I had no intention of going to Doris's. Doris was sleeping at Debbie Springfield's tonight, anyway.

"The stores are open until nine o'clock. We could go buy another sled," she said dreamily.

My father finally woke up.

"You shouldn't be sledding in your condition," he said. "Suppose you fall off the sled?"

"You're right," said Mom. My father heaved a sigh of relief and went into the kitchen to cut himself another piece of pizza.

"What I need," she continued thoughtfully, "is something with high sides that won't let me fall off. *I've got it!*" she shouted. "A cornflake carton! One of the big ones in the garage."

"You want to go sledding in one of those things?" asked Dad as he came back into the room.

"Come on, come on, it will be fun. Look at the moonlight on the snow. We may not have many more chances to sneak out spontaneously like this. Hortense will be okay, we'll just be out back. If she needs anything she can call to us, can't you, Hortense?"

"Oh, sure," I said. What a wacko.

"Come on, honey, where's your spirit of adventure?"

"Oh, all right," said Dad.

They put on boots and coats. I could hear them giggling together, and I caught a reference to Mr. Rabbit. Then they were gone. I sat in the den with the lights off so that I could see them. They climbed high to the top of the hill in the moonlight, and Dad helped Mom clamber into the carton. She hung on to the edge eagerly. Then he gave her a gentle push and swoosh, down she came, silently, swiftly in the moonlight. When she reached the bottom, she climbed out, stretched, and looked up the hill at Dad. He was looking down at her. I pulled the curtains and went to bed.

April

~~~~~~

I had hardly spoken to Doris all through March, but much good it did me. She didn't even notice. We sat on opposite sides of the lunchroom. She said hi to me in the halls at school and asked me over a few times, but I kept telling her I was busy. She must have known I wasn't busy, but she always said, "Okay." Finally I decided that she had suffered enough, and the next time she asked me over to play paper dolls, I agreed.

"So, how're the old ballet classes?" I said as we walked to her house after school.

It was slushy and I pretended I was keeping my eye out for puddles, so that I didn't have to look at her. Doris really was avoiding puddles. I didn't really care about her ballet classes, but I couldn't think of anything to say.

"I'm going to be in a recital next month," she said. "I am going to be the snowflake queen."

"The snowflake queen?" I'm sorry to say I giggled, but it couldn't be helped.

"What's so funny?" asked Doris.

"Doris, you have only been dancing for four months," I pointed out. "How come you are the snowflake queen?" I giggled again. I couldn't help it, all this ballet stuff was so dumb.

"I'm very talented. Next fall Mrs. Beddoe is going to put me in a special group of talented students."

"Oh, fah," I said.

"Debbie Springfield is going to start taking classes in the fall."

"Oh, really?" I said. This made me mad because while Debbie Springfield may be a raving beauty and Miss Perky Personality, her legs are, if anything, stumpier than mine.

We went into Doris's house. Doris asked her mother if we could have a cookie. If I asked my mother if I could have a cookie, my mother would think I had wigged out. In our house, if you want a cookie, you take a cookie. We carried our cookies and milk into the living room and got out the paper dolls. Somehow the joy had gone out of it. We had had a good paper doll story going—one of the girls was having a romance with one of the boys from the other set. The two families were very upset about it. When we had left them, no one was speaking to anyone else and the star-crossed paper dolls were having to sneak out to see each other. We set the dolls up as we had left them, but sometimes when you leave things for too long, you can't jump in again. You have to sort of warm up to it. To make matters worse, Debbie Springfield called.

"Darling," said Doris's mother, "it's Debbie."

Doris went to the phone in the kitchen and I could hear her giggling. When she came back, I had put the paper dolls away.

"I'd better go," I said.

"Okay," she said. "So do you want a ticket for my recital? I have to know in advance how many to reserve."

"Sure, I'll come if you want." I made it sound like I was doing her a big favor.

"Do you think your parents would like to come too?" she asked.

"Let's not get carried away," I said.

"Mr. and Mrs. Springfield are coming."

That certainly stumped me. "They must be hard up for entertainment. Nighty noodles," I said, and walked out.

I was so mad at Doris again that I wasn't looking where I was going and stepped plum into the middle of a freezing puddle. My tennis shoe was drenched and squished coldly all the way home, which just made me madder. As I got to the door I saw Aunt Kate getting into her car. I ran around to the passenger side, opened the door, and sat down. Aunt Kate turned in the driver's seat and looked at me expectantly.

"You know," I said, wondering if after all these months she was ready to be my confidante, "it is like musical chairs around here lately." I was in a reckless mood born of total exasperation and decided to plunge on. "You no longer see Barbara and Elise and see Mr. Baker instead. Letitia is no longer available for happy family parties because she is seeing Kathy or some other teenage friend. Doris is seeing Debbie Springfield. The old rabbit pals are wrapped up in the baby-to-be. I do not like the way things are going."

There was a silence as Aunt Kate looked at me as though she wasn't quite sure whether I had finished.

"Yeah, well," she said, dismissing me. "Some days are like that. Say, listen, Hortense, they're looking for kids to help out at the Eco Center. Why don't you volunteer?"

This was hardly what I would call sympathy. "Thanks a lot!" I shouted, slamming the car door on my way out.

Aunt Kate rolled down her window. "You're very welcome," she said politely, and drove off.

I thought that was just like Aunt Kate being all noble about *my* life. Why didn't *she* volunteer somewhere? Also, little did she know how many boxes of cornflakes I had given to charity in the last weeks.

I stamped into the house and went upstairs to take a hot bath before dinner. My mom was in the bathroom, painting it.

"I don't believe it," I said.

"What don't you believe, dear? Hortense, don't touch the wall!" she shrieked. "The paint is still wet."

"I don't believe you're painting the bathroom when you *promised* to paint my room next."

"I didn't promise. Remember, I said no promises. I had to paint the bathroom and recaulk it because of the mildew. I will do your room next."

"Oh no you won't," I yelled. "You'll do the living room or Letitia's room or Aunt Kate's room. Anything but my room, of course. You and Daddy don't care about me. Letitia never *did* like me. Aunt Kate wants me to *volunteer*. And Doris is a snowflake queen!"

I ran into my bedroom and slammed the door. I pushed my dresser in front of the door and jumped onto the bed and cried and cried. There is nothing like pulling out the stops and being completely miserable to make you feel good.

Mom kept knocking on the door and begging me to let her in and calling me Hortense honey, but I just told her to go peddle her papers somewhere else. Eventually she went away. The phone range, and Letitia knocked on my door to say it was for me, so then I had to come out. I wiped the tears off my face and limped downstairs. I had taken off my wet socks, but my foot was still red from the icy puddle.

I picked up the phone receiver. "Hello?"

"Hi," came a little voice. "Is this Hortense?"

"Yes," I said, wondering who in the world this was.

"This is Virginia Vermeulen."

"Oh."

"The thing is," she said, "you know, I see you around school a lot and in the orchard in the fall."

"Yeah?" I said. This was weird.

"You wanna sleep over at my house Friday night? It's my birthday." She added in a flat voice, "My mom is making a cake."

I didn't want to go over to her house. I was *scared* to go over to her house. The funny thing was that this voice on the phone didn't sound like Virginia Vermeulen, who everyone knew was a tramp who ate hot dogs for lunch and hung out with seventh-grade boys. I hadn't even spoken to her since February, when she talked to Doris and me at lunch. I don't know why I said yes, but I did. It seemed to surprise her as much as it did me. There was a big silence on the phone and then she just said, "Okay, see you then," in the same flat voice. I stood there stupidly holding the silent receiver in my hand. My mom came into the room and gave me a hug, but I shrugged it off. I was still mad about her not painting my room. It had been the last straw.

"I am going to sleep over at Virginia Vermeulen's Friday

night," I said. I hoped she would remember what I said about Virginia's being a tramp, and be a bit concerned, but all she said was "That's nice, dear."

"It's her birthday."

"Are you supposed to bring a present?" she asked.

"Yes," I said. I wanted to make her spend some money. She had gotten so tight lately.

"We'll go shopping tomorrow after school, shall we?" asked Mom.

"Just give me the money and I'll go myself," I said and turned on my heel to go upstairs to take a bath. I knew I was being really unpleasant, but I didn't care.

The next day, when I saw Virginia at school, we didn't even speak to each other. I didn't speak to Doris, either. Suddenly I wasn't speaking to anyone. After school I went downtown to Woolworth's with the money Mom had given me. What to buy for Virginia? She wasn't the game type as far as I could tell. I didn't think we had exactly the same taste in clothes, so that was out. Finally I bought her some gardenia bubble bath like Letitia's. Letitia always uses sophisticated stuff, so I figured at least Virginia wouldn't think it was a babyish present. I got some wrapping paper and a card, too.

Friday night, Dad dropped me off at the Vermeulens'. I felt really nervous. I hadn't talked to Virginia all week. I made my dad wait in the car at the foot of the driveway with the lights out. That way, if it was a practical joke, I would have a ride. Or if maybe a gang of seventh-grade boys was hiding, waiting to ambush me, I would have an escape. On the other hand, if Virginia was serious, she wouldn't see my dad waiting in the car, which would make me look like I expected an ambush or something.

Virginia met me at the door. I stretched my right arm over my head, a signal for Dad to take a powder. She was still dressed awfully. Apparently she didn't tone things down at home. She was wearing a purple T-shirt with the sleeves cut out, patched blue jeans, yellow leg warmers, and a green bandanna tied around her neck.

"Hi," she said, "what's happening?"

What could I say to that? I was here because she had invited me. That was what was happening.

"Hi," I said.

"Have your little friend come in," said Virginia's mother somewhere in the background. To mothers everywhere your friends are always little. It is disgusting. Then I saw Virginia's mother, and I guessed everyone was little to her by sheer comparison. Her stomach stuck out a mile.

"How do you do, Hortense?" asked Virginia's mom, shaking my hand.

I had seen her at the farm, but I had never actually met her. She had a fascinating voice, sort of like a bullfrog and sort of like a foghorn. It was not unpleasant. She was wearing a tattered gray dress. I guessed they didn't have much money. Their house was pretty beat up and there weren't any rugs on the floor. Mom would have gone crazy painting in their house. There were parts of the wall where the paint had peeled off and no one had even bothered to slap a picture over the bald spots or anything. Three of Virginia's little brothers were racing around on the linoleum with trucks, making a bunch of noise. Virginia just ignored them.

"Do you want to see my room?" asked Virginia. "Well, actually I share it with my sister, but she's going to sleep on the couch tonight."

"Sure," I said, and we went through a dim hall and up

some dark stairs to her tiny room. It was about half the size of my room and had just enough space for two small beds and a dresser. I put down my overnight bag and then, because I didn't know what to do, I got her present out of my bag and handed it to her. "Here. Happy birthday."

"Oh, gosh," said Virginia. "You didn't have to do that."

"I hope you like it," I said lamely.

She opened it. "Gee. Bubble bath." She sounded genuinely pleased. "I've never had any bubble bath." She unscrewed the cap and smelled it. "It smells good, too. Gee, thanks."

We sat down on the beds, facing each other. "To tell you the truth," she said, "I didn't think you'd come. I mean, whenever I try to talk to you at school, you always run away."

"Oh," I said. This was embarrassing.

"Like, you know, the time I tried to tell you my mom was pregnant, too."

"Well, you're always hanging out with those seventh-grade boys," I said, deciding to lay my cards on the table.

"Bob and Gene and Roy? So what? I've been hanging out with them since we were born practically. The problem with living way out here is that there aren't any girls close enough to play with. I kept hoping a family with girls would buy one of the neighboring farms. But Bob and Gene and Roy are real nice. I mean, a lot of guys wouldn't let a girl play with them."

I felt kind of like a jerk. "So your mom is going to have a baby, huh?"

"In July. When is your mom going to have the baby?"

"June. I'll be glad when it's all over. She's been completely impossible," I said, leaning back against the wall and putting my feet up and trying to sound tougher than I am. I am not

by nature "cool." I don't think anyone who has read *Little
Women* seven times can hope to be cool, but I can fake it if
I have to.

"Yeah? My mom is the way she's always been, only more
worried. I hope it's a girl. All my sisters are older, and with
three little brothers, a little sister might be nice for a change.
What do you hope your mom has?"

"Oh, it will be a girl. My family only has girls," I said.

"I never heard of that before," she said. "How come?"

"I don't know."

"Well, you're lucky. Boys are a pain in the neck."

"Except for Roy and Gene and Bob?" I said.

"Right," she said. "But lately, to tell you the truth, they've
been leaving me out a lot. I think they're getting razzed at
school for playing with me. After dinner, do you want to go
behind the barn and smoke a cherry cigar?"

"Sure," I said. I hoped my mom knew what she had driven
me to.

Virginia reached under her bed and pulled out a package
of cherry cigars. She pulled up her leg warmer and blue
jeans and hid them in the top of her knee sock. "Roy gave
me these," she said. "I think he feels rotten that they don't
play with me as much anymore." Just then her mom called
us for dinner, and we ran downstairs.

They had a huge kitchen, and a huge kitchen table ran
down the middle of it. There were nine of them altogether.
Mr. Vermeulen had a florid face and big rough, red hands.
I sat next to him, and every time he passed me something I
couldn't help but stare at them.

"So how are you, Hortense?" he asked me.

"Just fine, thank you," I said.

He laughed, but I don't know why. It was a big belly laugh.

Virginia's mother kept pushing her bulky self out of the chair to run and get things from the stove, refill bowls, pour milk, and wipe off Virginia's youngest brother, who had food smeared from ear to ear. I would lose my appetite and shrink away to nothing if I had to eat with him every night. Everyone was talking very noisily, and Virginia and I chatted to each other like no one else was at the table.

We compared notes on people we knew. I told her Doris was seeing Debbie Springfield.

"She thinks she's so cute," I said of Debbie.

"Well, she is," said Virginia. "If I were that cute I would think I was cute, too."

"I can't imagine what she sees in Doris," I said.

"What do you?" asked Virginia, not nastily but just like she was kind of interested. "I mean, maybe she sees the same thing."

It seemed to me that Virginia was turning out to be not at all the type of person she appeared to be. I thought she was a walk on the wild side, but here she was sounding like the voice of reason.

I looked around as Virginia's father passed me the chicken. Virginia's little brother kept beating on the table with a spoon and spilling milk and throwing mashed potatoes, and no one said boo to him. I thought about Doris's family. They were so much neater than my family that I always thought we were real slobs. As I ate with this family, it occurred to me that my family was almost persnickety in its neatness.

Then Virginia's mom brought out a cake and we all sang "Happy Birthday." After dessert, Mrs. Vermeulen excused Virginia from the dishes. Her father got a beer out of the refrigerator and her brothers started playing with their trucks again. Virginia and I went out behind the barn to smoke the cherry cigar.

It was a balmy night and much darker here in the country than it was around our house with the well-lit streets and the close-together houses. There were old, crackling leaves and dry grass on the lawn from last fall. We leaned against the barn. The sky was a million stars. Virginia lit the cigar, took a puff, and handed it to me. I took a puff. It tasted exotic, if terrible.

"Ugh," I said.

"Haven't you ever smoked a cherry cigar before?" asked Virginia.

"No," I said. "Do you *like* them?"

"I've never smoked one before either. Live and learn," she said, stamping it out on the ground.

We looked up at the sky. You couldn't help it. The sky was a huge bowl of twinkling, moving dots. It seemed to pull you upward. To think what I missed every night. I never wanted to go in.

"My dad smokes cigars," I said.

"Ummm," said Virginia. "Look over there, there's Cassiopeia. Do you know how to find the North Star? You just go to those stars on the Big Dipper, they're called the Pointers, and then you follow the line out." She traced this with her finger. "To there. That's the North Star."

"Wow," I said. "Who taught you that?"

"My dad. He knows all about the stars. I'm saving up for a telescope. I love studying the stars. But at the rate I'm going, I'll be about a hundred years old by the time I get one."

"How much allowance do you get?" I asked.

"I don't get an allowance. Listen, if my mom and dad gave

us all allowances, they'd be broke. I pick apples and grapes in the fall, and in a couple of years I'm going to start baby-sitting."

I kept wondering where she got the money for hot dogs if she didn't get an allowance. I didn't ask her, though.

"Anyhow, for Christmas I got a book about astronomy. There's a big book at the bookstore about the stars that I want because it's got great pictures, and maybe I'll buy that and then the telescope."

"Why don't you just go to the library?" I asked.

"We don't belong," she said.

"Well, it doesn't cost anything. You can join all by yourself, if you want. Tomorrow, why don't you come with me to the library and I'll show you how to get a card. Then you can get all the books you want."

Her mother appeared on the doorstep calling us, and we went into the house.

"It's getting late, Virginia," she said and leaned down to kiss her. "Happy birthday."

Virginia squirmed. I would have died if my mom had kissed me in front of Doris like that. We went upstairs and put on our nightgowns. She had a regular nightgown. I mean, it wasn't all purple and lime green like her clothes. But it was really tattered. My mother would never let me wear a tattered nightgown like that. We lay in bed and stared at the ceiling.

"You ever play with paper dolls?" I asked her.

"No," she said.

I decided I liked her anyway.

The next morning, Virginia and I got up and had breakfast. You can imagine my feelings at seeing a box of cornflakes looming at me, but luckily they had Wheaties, too. Her little brothers were eating in the kitchen and they were disgusting. They had cereal all over their chins. We took our cereal out to the front porch.

The birds were loud and the sun had the golden, rosy look of early morning. We rocked on their old wood and leather rocking chairs. I wondered what it would be like to get up and sit out there every morning.

"It must be inspirational sitting out here in the morning," I said and then worried that I had overdone my poetic observations just a bit.

Virginia nodded, crunching away. "Yes, I get up and think about how I am going to make enough money for a telescope."

She certainly seemed to be obsessed with that telescope.

"Listen, Virginia," I said, "if you are trying to save up for a telescope, then what are you doing buying hot dogs for lunch every day?"

"That is my oasis," she said. "My mom says everyone needs an oasis in their day every day. For her, it's a bath. Every day she takes a bath for half an hour, and no one can disturb her for anything. For my sister Meg, it's a cup of coffee by herself on the front porch. My mom didn't want her to drink coffee until she was older, but the rule is that you pick your own oasis within reason, and everyone has to accommodate it. My dad gets a beer in front of the TV after dinner. For me, it's hot-dog money. I don't get an allowance, so the only way I can sneak out of school for hot dogs is if my mom gives me hot-dog money. Naturally, I am honor-bound to spend it only on hot dogs. I need a lunchtime oasis because I hate school."

This was a shocker. I never thought of anyone hating

school before. Of course, I knew such people existed, but I never expected to like one of them.

"You hate school?" I asked.

"I just hate being cooped up."

"Let's go to the library," I said.

We got my stuff and I called my dad. He picked us up and drove us to my house, where I left my things.

Before we left, I sneaked into the garage and put a couple of boxes of cornflakes in my knapsack to drop off at the food depot by the library. I had made quite a dent in our supply these last weeks. I explained to Virginia what I was doing and why.

She laughed. "Isn't your mother going to notice that all the cornflakes are suddenly gone?"

"Ha!" I said. "Her attention is elsewhere these days, to say the least! Hurry or we'll miss our bus."

We ran to the bus stop.

When we got to the library, I walked Virginia up to the front desk, but she grabbed my sleeve and pulled me back.

"What?" I asked.

"Shhh. Shhh," she whispered and pulled me over to the periodicals. I don't know why they call the magazines the "periodicals." It must be just something the library does to maintain its dignity.

"Do you need identification to get a library card?"

"This is a library," I said. "Crooks don't come to a library. Only honorable people get library cards. Of course you don't need identification."

"In that case, let's think up a phony name for my library card," she said.

"What?"

"Let's think up a phony name. Let's get a bunch of cards out in different names."

"Why?" I asked, frankly shocked.

"For fun. I hate the name Virginia. What difference does it make? I'm not going to steal any books. I'd just like to be Moira Egan Amanda McPherson for a change. What's the matter, you never wanted to be anyone but Hortense Hemple?"

"What if they found out?"

"What if they did? Why should they care what name is on your card as long as you give them the right address and return your books on time? Haven't you ever heard of a nom de plume?"

I was sure there was something wrong with this, but as I was trying to figure out what, I spied Debbie Springfield and Doris sitting in the reading room together. How cozy. I left Virginia standing by the periodicals, where she had gotten sidetracked by a *National Geographic* with pictures of the moon.

"So," I said, boldly marching right up to them.

"Hi, Hortense," said Doris.

"So?"

"We're doing our social studies project together."

"Oh, yeah?" I said. "Well, I finished my social studies project a week ago."

"You still haven't picked up your ticket for my ballet recital," said Doris.

"Good thing too," I replied evenly, "because I need two. Virginia and I are going together."

"Virginia who?" asked Doris.

"Virginia Vermeulen."

"Don't make me laugh," said Doris.

"What's so funny?" I asked. "If you must know, we have become pretty tight."

Debbie whispered something to Doris. This was so rude that I instinctively rose above it. They giggled. I decided not to say anything but lifted my nose in the air reprovingly. There is nothing more maddening to Doris than to feel she is being risen above.

"See you," I said politely.

Doris and Debbie began giggling again, and the reference room librarian said "Shh," I am happy to say.

"Jane Louise Smith," I said to Virginia, pulling her to the washroom so we could finish discussing this.

"Jane Smith?" she asked.

"I want something plain," I said positively. "Not Rowena Matilda or Maxine or Geraldina or Evangeline or Hortense or Letitia. Jane Smith."

Virginia nodded acceptingly. "Okay, I'm going with Moira Egan Amanda McPherson. This week."

We approached the desk. I told the girl we wanted to get library cards, and she gave us two blank cards to fill out with our names and addresses and the next of kin.

"In case we keel over in the periodicals," whispered Virginia.

When we had finished, she passed them to another woman, who typed up our library cards, and that was all there was to it.

I was surprised at how easy it was, but our branch of the Riverside Public Library was still pretty low-tech and trusted in the innate honesty of the bookworm. I felt guilty and wanted to run out, but Virginia still wanted to get some books. When she saw how many books they had on astronomy, she practically foamed at the mouth.

"You can only get two books on any subject," I said. "But you can get five fiction and five non-fiction all together."

Well, I can only say that she ran amok after that. She chose two astronomy books after taking half an hour to decide. It was only when I pointed out to her that she could read them this week and come back next week for two more that she could be pulled away. I got my two Edward Eagers and three non–Edward Eagers and explained to her my theory of brain progression as we sat on the library steps. It was a warm and sunny day. There was a craft fair in the park, and I could see the vendors hawking cold drinks—the kind that drizzle forever down the sides of the drink machines in orange and purple liquid invitation. They are always ultimately disappointing. I think the disappointment stems from the fact that once in the cup, the liquid stays put.

Balloons were being blown up and put on sticks. There was that faint new-mown-lawn smell in the air.

"Of course," I continued, "when I have reread the Edward Eagers, I have to branch out for a few weeks and reread *Pippi Longstocking,* or E. Nesbit, or Louisa May Alcott or *Baby Island* or *The Saturdays* or *Mrs. Piggle-Wiggle.* Sometimes, in the interest of brain progression, I will find a new author like Louise Fitzhugh, but usually it's dull going."

"I don't care so much about brain progression myself," said Virginia. "I like my brain where it is. I'd be afraid it would progress to a place I didn't like."

"Hmmm," I said. I had never considered this.

"Want to go to the museum?" I asked.

The second floor over the library was the Riverside Museum. It was free. It had a mummy, some Indian artifacts, and exhibits on what Riverside was like in pioneer days. I especially liked the gift shop, where you could get rocks,

stuff from Mexico, fans, dolls from many countries, or my
favorite, surprise balls, which you had to unwrap and unwrap to reveal the trinket. Usually I can't afford anything
from the gift shop because of a certain penchant for licorice
whips.

Virginia had never been to the museum. This was one
underprivileged kid. We wandered through and then looked
at the stuff in the gift shop, and Virginia asked the woman
behind the counter if they had any telescopes. The woman
smiled and said no, but that next to the museum was the
planetarium. So we went there next. It turned out that it cost
two dollars to get in, which was beyond our meager means,
but Virginia said she was going to mow lawns all week and
get enough money to come back. Then we went to the craft
show, which was free. I bought Virginia and myself a drink.
She had grape and I had orange. We drank half and then
mixed the two remaining halves together to see what it
would be like. This was Virginia's idea.

"I am always looking for an invention that will make me
a million dollars," she said. "I don't care about a lavish life-
style, I only want—"

"I know, I know," I said. "A telescope."

"I don't think the grape and orange drink is going to make
you a million," I said after a pause.

"I don't think so either," she said, but finished it anyway.

I wished I had enough money left to buy us both ice
creams, too, but my allowance can only be stretched so far.
Instead, I bought one of the helium balloons on a stick.

"Here," I said, giving it to Virginia. "No birthday is com-
plete without one."

We sat next to the fountain, where we could feel the spray.
Then I told her about *my* birthday.

"How crappy," she said. "Your relatives sound like raving lunatics. Imagine bringing baby presents to your birthday! I've never heard of anything so tacky in my life."

"That's it!" I said. "That's exactly what I thought. It was so *tacky*."

We sat there and swung our legs and watched people go by the rest of the afternoon. It was the best Saturday I ever had.

May

~~~~~~

*T*he first two weeks of May, I was very busy with Virginia. We mowed lawns after school until we had enough money to go to the planetarium together. I was frankly bored, getting a crick in my neck staring at what was supposed to be a bunch of stars. It wasn't at all like looking at the *real* stars, if you ask me. It didn't seem to matter to Virginia, who left the building sighing and clasping her hands.

It was a beautiful May day. The tulips and daffodils were in bloom. Great patches of blooming bushes burst out at us. The lilacs and fruit trees perfumed the air, which had that heavy pollen-and-dew-laden feeling that makes you move slowly.

After the planetarium we went back to Virginia's and sat on the porch swing and ate Twinkies. Mrs. Vermeulen was down by the barn, waddling around.

"I don't know why we are even going to this stupid recital

tonight," I said to Virginia. "I have broken forever my ties with Doris. Why should she think I would want to see her as some dumb snowflake queen?"

"Oh, well," said Virginia languidly. "We already have the tickets. Your parents sprang for them, so we're not out of pocket."

"I suppose," I said sulkily, licking the creamy stuff from the Twinkie cellophane.

"And we can stay out late. If the recital starts at eight, I doubt we'll be out of there until ten o'clock, and with a little finagling, I bet I can get my dad to take us to Dairy Queen on the way home."

"It's a thought," I said, perking up. My parents were dropping us off, and Virginia's were picking us up.

I went home at about four o'clock to change and eat dinner. Aunt Kate and my mom were sitting at the kitchen table together. Mom looked hot and was panting. Aunt Kate was drumming her fingers and saying, "Okay, now pant, blow." I knew they were only doing my mother's silly breathing exercises, but they looked as if something was on their minds, too.

"Now what?" I asked.

"Hurry and get changed into something to wear to Doris's recital," said my mom. "Daddy is taking you to McDonald's for dinner, and you won't have time afterward."

I made faces at Aunt Kate behind her back. I had not forgiven her for dismissing me when I had tried to confide in her. Unfortunately, Aunt Kate caught me making a particularly horrible face and followed me upstairs.

"What's your problem?" she asked.

Ha! As if I'd tell *you,* I wanted to say. I did not say this because I found myself cowed as always by Aunt Kate. I maintained a dignified if sulky silence.

"I'm sorry if I hurt your feelings when I suggested you volunteer for the Eco Center. That *is* what this is about, isn't it?" said Aunt Kate crisply.

"Perhaps," I said coolly.

"But if there's one thing I can't stand, it's people emoting all over the place. Let us just bury the whole matter as though it never happened," she said like this more than took care of things, and went back downstairs, leaving me staring at her open-mouthed. She could have at least let me nobly forgive her.

I ran into my room and put on the dress that Aunt Kate had given me for my birthday. When I came down the stairs, Aunt Kate was drumming her fingers again. My mom was staring out our back kitchen window.

"You'd better take a raincoat, Hortense," she said. "I don't like the look of those clouds in the southwest."

I looked out the window and could see what she meant. The whole top of the sky was dark.

"Is there a tornado watch on?" I asked.

We usually get the tornadoes from the southwest. There are a few alarms every spring and summer. I am terrified of tornadoes, and if there is a watch on, I won't go out if I can help it. They say you can go about your business and only have to worry if there is a warning, which means one has been spotted, either hanging in the clouds, or touching down—a phrase that really strikes terror into my heart, as I can just see the evil funnel reaching the ground and heading straight for us all. They say it makes the sound of a train, but by the time you hear it or see it, it is too late. That's how fast it moves.

"No watch on yet," said my mother. "It sure looks like there should be, doesn't it? It's certainly tornado weather."

In tornado weather, the sky is black, and the air has a

yellowy greenish color and feels hazy and heavy. I could still hear the birds, though. During true tornado weather, everything becomes silent, like someone suddenly turned the sound off the TV but left the picture running. That's when I head for the basement.

Daddy and Letitia came into the kitchen, and we all went out to the car.

"Hey, isn't Mom coming?" I asked.

"I think she's a little tired," said Dad lamely. I mean, there's nothing so taxing about going to get burgers, is there?

"I smell trouble," I whispered to Letitia in the back seat.

"Trouble?" said Letitia loudly. She never learns.

"What kind of trouble?" asked my dad.

"Nothing," I said. I waited until Dad was inside McDonald's to bring it up again. I always make everyone eat in the car. I can be very persuasive when I like.

"Mom and Aunt Kate looked worried when I came in."

"So?" said Letitia.

"Something is afoot," I said. "But where does the trouble lie? With Mom or Aunt Kate?"

"Aunt Kate," said Letitia airily and blew a bubble with her gum.

"How do you know?" I asked, clutching her arm eagerly.

"Because I was eavesdropping," said Letitia. "I was taking a bath and I heard about half of what they said."

"Well?"

"Aunt Kate is buying this cabin up north and is trying to decide whether to live there permanently."

"The plot thickens," I said. I didn't know if I wanted her to go. I had come to rely on her giving the family a little pizzazz.

"Do you think she is trying to escape the baby?" I asked.

"More likely it has something to do with this heavy romance with Old Crazy Joe," said Letitia.

"You know about that?" I asked. I thought I alone shared this secret with Aunt Kate.

"It would be hard not to know about it," said Letitia. "Everyone sees them out together. She takes off up north to fish with him every weekend. Where have you been?"

"Naturally *I* knew. I am, after all, Aunt Kate's special friend."

"I thought Joe was Aunt Kate's special friend," said Letitia and sniggered.

"Gee, maybe they'll get married," I said.

"Fat chance," said Letitia.

"Why not?"

"Because Aunt Kate's got more sense. Only wimpy women who can't take care of themselves get married. Marriage is nothing more than enslavement. I have decided I am never going to marry."

"What about Mom?"

"What *about* Mom? I hate to tell you, Hortense dear, but your mother, though possessing many endearing qualities, is not too tightly wrapped."

I thought about this. "Oh, pooh," I said finally. "She may be a little ditsy, well, worse since she got pregnant, I grant you, but deep down she's got a lot of sense. I think all this rabbit business is just affected."

I thought it would have been nice to pursue this discussion, but just then my dad returned with our hamburgers. I didn't want to discuss this around my dad. He likes to think Letitia and I are two happy innocents, and I don't want to disabuse him of this idea.

We finished the last slurps of our milk shakes and headed

home silently. We dropped Letitia off and went to get Virginia. She was wearing yellow jeans, tennis shoes, a green baseball shirt, and a big orange ribbon in her hair. Sometimes I am ashamed to be seen with her.

"Don't you own a dress?" I asked.

"Of course I own a dress," she said, getting into the car. "Hello, Mr. Hemple," she said to my dad. "How are you?"

"Just fine, Virginia," said Dad. He likes Virginia because most kids my age are shy around grownups but Virginia isn't afraid of anyone. "How are you?"

"I'm fine. Do *you* think I should have worn a dress, Mr. Hemple?" she asked.

"I think you look simply ravishing," said my father.

"There, you see?" said Virginia. "You don't want to overdress for this affair. You don't want Doris to think this is a big occasion for *you.*"

"Oh, I see." Now I wished I had worn jeans too.

"I betcha we get a tornado," she said. "Don't you think it looks ripe for a tornado, Mr. Hemple?" That's another thing about Virginia. She always includes the driving grownup in the conversation instead of treating him or her like the chauffeur.

"Well, I don't know," said Dad. "A cold front's moving in and that could be trouble."

"Why is that?" she asked.

"Why, that's how tornadoes are formed. A cold front and a warm front meet and the cold front is on top. Well, the cold front wants to get down and the warm front wants to get up, so the warm air pushes up and the cold air pushes down and in the tension a funnel is formed."

"You don't say," said Virginia. "I never knew that. I just thought tornadoes came in the spring, like forsythia. What did you think, Hortense?"

"I don't know," I said.

I was embarrassed to tell her that I didn't really believe this scientific explanation of tornadoes. To me, tornadoes are evil spirits that are always there just waiting until spring to burst out and frighten the bejesus out of you. They're loud, terrifying, and kin to the monsters that live under the bed.

We pulled up in front of the school.

"So long, girls. Have a nice time," said my dad. "Now, Virginia's parents are picking you up, right?"

"Don't worry if we're a little late," said Virginia. "We are going to try to con my dad into taking us for ice cream afterward."

"Well, here, then," said Dad, getting out his wallet and handing me ten dollars. "You treat, Hortense."

"You don't have to do that, Mr. Hemple," said Virginia.

"Never mind," said Dad. "This one's on me. Bye-bye, girls. Have fun." And he drove off.

We went in and settled ourselves in one of the middle rows. There were already a lot of people there. I scrunched down in my seat. I don't know why, but whenever I am in a theater, I feel like everyone is looking at me. After a few minutes, I sat up a bit more and surreptitiously peered around. Virginia was reading her program.

"Do you see Debbie Springfield?" I whispered to her.

She looked around frankly. I never understand how people can do this.

"Nope," she said in a loud voice. "I guess they haven't come yet. Hey, look, Doris is the second act on the program. Snowflakes and snowflake queen."

"Shh," I said loudly.

"What's the matter?" she whispered.

"Nothing, nothing," I said, hunkering down farther in my seat.

"Why are you hiding?" asked Virginia.

"Everyone is looking at us."

"No one is paying any attention to us," said Virginia sensibly. "Look, they're all busy talking to each other. Want to put our programs on our seats and go out for a drink of water?"

We went into the hall and found the drinking fountain. It was right by the dressing room. Doris and her parents were standing there. I bent over the fountain with Virginia blocking me.

"Don't move," I hissed. "The last thing I want to do is talk to Doris or her family."

"Okay," hissed back Virginia.

"Now, Doris," said Mrs. Gunderson in her twangy voice, "you're not nervous, are you?"

"No," said Doris in a meek tone.

"There's no reason to be nervous. Even if you make a mistake, no one will care. Daddy and I will be right there watching. You may not be able to see us because there will be lots of people in the audience, but we'll be there."

"Uh," said Doris in a sick voice.

"If you do forget the steps, just make something up. No one will ever know the difference."

"Ooooh," moaned Doris.

"You're not getting stage fright, are you, Doris?" she asked anxiously.

"What's that?" asked Doris, sounding more and more scared.

"It's the fear of performing."

"How does it feel?" asked Doris.

"I don't really know, dear," said Doris's mom musingly. "I guess your mouth goes all dry and you get butterflies in your stomach and your heart races and your mind goes blank."

"Oh, no!" said Doris, and all in a second my bad feelings for her were gone and I felt sorry for her instead. Her mother was really a dope. I knew that if Doris didn't have stage fright before, she sure had it now. I also knew that I was glad she had found Debbie Springfield. I was tired of being the one to buck her up. Let Debbie do it for a while. Also, if Doris hadn't found Debbie, I might never have found Virginia.

The Gundersons moved into the dressing room, and Virginia and I went back and sat down. Finally people began filling up the auditorium, and the lights flickered and went down. The curtain rose and out tripped a bunch of tiny tots in tutus. They were pretty funny, stumbling around the stage, but Virginia and I just smiled at each other and didn't laugh the way a couple of lugs two rows back did. The applause was tumultuous.

Next the music started again and out came a bunch of snowflakes with white net tutus and feathery hairpieces. They floated about and then stood still for Doris's entrance as the snowflake queen. She looked okay, and I had to hand it to her, she was the best dancer there: her legs were longer and her feet pointier and her arms more snowflake-like than any of the others'. She circled the dancing snowflakes and rose gradually onto one leg. Suddenly she stopped moving. She simply stopped, her mouth fell open, and she stared bug-eyed at the audience. I knew the dreaded stage fright was upon her. The other snowflakes were tippy-toeing off the stage, which would have been fine if Doris had continued dancing, but given her stricken condition, it looked embarrassingly like they were sneaking away. The music went on and on. You could tell that this should have been the big snowflake queen solo, but the snowflake queen was frozen to the floor.

"Make something up," you could hear someone whispering in the wings.

I couldn't bear to watch any more and was just closing my eyes when an announcement came over the P.A. At first I thought it was a stage direction for poor old Doris. So did she, evidently, because her eyes got even bigger and she jumped about two feet in the air, her first movement for many minutes.

"Ladies and gentlemen," came the voice, "I'm sorry to interrupt this evening's performance, but the weather bureau has just issued a tornado warning for southwest Michigan. Two tornadoes have touched down in Allegan County, and all surrounding counties are advised to take shelter. Please exit the theater in an orderly fashion."

The lights snapped back on and Virginia and I got up. I was shaking.

"Come on, come on," I said, pulling Virginia's sleeve. I didn't know what to do. Should we beg a ride with Doris's family? Virginia's family wouldn't be here until ten. Maybe we should phone my family; they lived closer.

"Calm down," said Virginia. "I bet Daddy is in the parking lot right now. I'm sure they heard the weather warning, too."

"We'd better phone." I started to drag her through the mill of people to a telephone. "Where's a phone? Where's a darn phone? Oh, my gosh, I don't have any change."

Virginia grabbed me and pulled me to the parking lot. Both of our dads were there, eyeing the crowd, trying to spot us. "Over here," she called to them. "I told you so," she said to me. "See you tomorrow."

She ran to her dad and I ran to mine.

"Thank goodness," I said, breathing hard and jumping in the front seat. "Hurry."

"For goodness' sake," he said, "relax. The tornado isn't even headed this way. The warning is just a precaution."

"Yeah, but they're sounding the siren. We've got to *get to the basement.*"

"We'll get there soon enough. How was the performance?"

"Okay," I said and chewed my nails. I was in no mood for idle chitchat. I listened to the eerie one-note wail of the siren.

When we got home, Mom and Letitia were in the basement, listening to the radio. They didn't know where Aunt Kate was. I ran down and sat scrunched against one wall. Our basement isn't finished, so it was no fun sitting there on the grubby cement.

"Where's Daddy?" asked Mom.

"I don't know," I said. "I thought he was right behind me." We waited and waited, but he didn't appear.

"Dad?" I called.

"I'll go up and see," said Letitia.

"Don't go up there!" I yelled. "The tornado may be coming and by the time you see it, it is *too late.*"

"Well, don't you want to know where Daddy is?" asked Letitia.

"I'll go see," said Mom.

"You stay right there," I said. She was so big and fat that she would never get down the stairs in time if chased by a tornado.

"I'll go," I said. I felt safer directing operations. I was quite certain no one else had enough sense. If anyone was going to protect this family from tornadoes, it would have to be me.

I ran up the stairs. "Dad?" I called.

"Out here," he said. I found him sitting on our back steps, smoking a pipe and looking toward the southwest.

"What are you doing?" I shouted.

"I've always wanted to see a tornado. If we're going to have one, I would hate to miss it."

"You fool," I said. I was so disturbed that I didn't even think about hurting his feelings. "Don't you realize that by the time you *see* it, it will be too late?"

"Don't worry, Hortense, as soon as I get a good look at it, I will run to the basement."

"Daddy, please come down to the basement."

"Run along, Hortense." He laughed. "I promise I won't stay out here a moment longer than necessary. Hear how quiet it's gotten? Interesting clouds out there, too. See the black wisps coming down out of those thunderheads?"

"Please come downstairs, Daddy," I begged.

"Okay, I will, soon," he said.

I didn't like leaving him there, but I heard sounds in the kitchen. Mom had waddled up and was fixing a big bowl of cornflakes.

"Oh, no, not *now*," I said. "Get downstairs."

"Hortense," she said.

"THIS INSTANT," I roared, and she scuttled down, taking the bowl with her.

I followed her down. Letitia had turned the radio from the weather watch to a rock 'n' roll station in Detroit.

"Oh, my God," I said. I grabbed the radio and turned it back.

"Hey!" protested Letitia.

"Hortense is right," said Mom. "Leave the station to the weather. If you want to listen to rock 'n' roll, get your Walkman."

Letitia went upstairs.

"Hurry, hurry, hurry," I said, following her up. As she was getting her Walkman, Aunt Kate appeared at the door.

"Quick, get into the basement," I said.

"Calm down," said Aunt Kate.

"Where have you been?" I asked.

"I was out walking, and when I heard the siren, I headed home. What are you, the disaster monitor?"

"Well, *someone* has to be," I snapped and shooed Aunt Kate down the stairs.

"Letitia, what's taking so long?" I yelled at her. She came down with her earphones on and went back to the basement. I could hear thunder in the southwest.

I wanted to go to the basement, too, but I couldn't leave Dad out on the porch alone. He may not realize it, but he was no longer so young and spry. If a tornado came, I couldn't trust him to get downstairs in time. He might even freeze with fear. I would have to wait it out with him. I sat on the swing, and we stared to the southwest together with no sound but the oompah-oompah pull of his pipe.

"Watch," he said and blew three smoke rings. I tapped my foot. There was no wind, only that quiet heavy haze and the low rumble of thunder. Lightning flashed across the sky. He oompahed and I tapped for an hour until my mother appeared.

"They've lifted the warning," she said. "There's just a watch on now."

My father sighed. "Shoot," he said. "I thought I'd finally get a chance to see a tornado."

I went wearily to bed. Sometimes they really exasperate me.

June

~~~~~~

*I*n June two things happened: the weather got hot and our house shrank. A heavy wave of heat and humidity settled over Riverside, so that we were all in need of palmetto fans and mint juleps, whatever those are. Aunt Kate kept murmuring about her pith helmet. Letitia and Kathy had suddenly acquired a pack of weasels who were hoping to win them over with their oafish charms, I guess. I wouldn't have cared except that after spending the entire winter at Kathy's house, Kathy and Letitia had apparently decided to use our house as their summer residence. They hung out in the living room, and when they were there we were not allowed within spitting distance. Letitia wouldn't even let us use the dining room because it connects to the living room and has no door and someone might get a glimpse of us and realize that we *live with her.*

Aunt Kate and Mom and I were huddled in the kitchen Saturday morning, drinking lemonade and listening glumly to the weather report, when the telephone rang. Mom heaved herself out of her chair to answer it. I decided that if she got much bigger, we would have to buy her a crane.

My mom picked up the phone and made those fake cheerful noises you make when you are trying to hide your total revulsion.

"What do you know? That was your father's cousin Jake from Kentucky, and he's on vacation and just happens to be in town."

"I hope you suggested a good motel," said Aunt Kate. "I hear the Beehive is quite reasonable."

"Naturally I invited him to stay with us."

"Where are you going to put him? In the nursery?"

"I guess Letitia and Hortense will have to double up for a couple of nights."

"Oh, no," I said. Not that it would be such a big deal sleeping in Letitia's room, but I hate strange houseguests hanging around.

"Did he say how long he was staying?" asked Aunt Kate.

"Not exactly," said my mother, biting her nails.

"You should have asked," said Aunt Kate. "Particularly if you don't know this guy very well. Pin him down from the beginning."

"How long can it be? If he's on vacation, I'm sure Riverside doesn't interest him. Surely he's only passing through?"

"Harrumph," said Aunt Kate and got to her feet and went up to her room.

Virginia and I spent the day at the library. It had become too warm to mow lawns, and the library was air-conditioned. Virginia had discovered a magazine called *Astronomer's Monthly* that she couldn't check out. I read next to her in the periodicals until I got bored and then nipped over to

the Chocolate Shop for a cherry phosphate, which has re-
markable restorative powers.

When I got home at four o'clock, Jake, Mom, and Dad
were all sitting in the kitchen. The weasel pack were with
Kathy and Letitia in the living room. I couldn't believe that
Mom wasn't even kicking out the pack for visiting potentates.

"Hortense dear," said my mother, with an awful ghastly
smile smeared across her plump face, "this is your father's
cousin Jake. This is my youngest, Jake," she said.

"Not for long. Ho ho ho," sniggered Jake. He was wearing
mud-colored pants with suspenders and a very dirty T-shirt.

"How do you do?" I asked politely.

"Well, I *do* jest fine," he said. "And how do you do de do
de do? Ho ho ho."

My father winced.

"Jake used to be a guide at Mammoth Cave," said Dad.

"Uh huh," I said. We took a trip there once. It is this huge
cave in Kentucky. Frankly, I didn't think there was much to
see. A cave is a cave, and a mammoth cave is just a big one.

"I don't work there no more," said Jake.

"Oh," I said.

"I quit," he said. "Know why?"

I shook my head.

"Bat attack." He sat back waiting for a reaction.

"I see," I said.

"Jake was attacked by a bat," said my mother as though I
weren't quite bright.

"Yup. Went right for my hair. They say bats don't go for
your hair, but that's what he did, the bugger, went right for
my hair. Big thing, too." Jake spread his arms wide. "That
big. No kidding."

Aunt Kate drifted in through the back door.

"Kate, this is Jake," said my mother.

Jake stood up and extended a grimy hand. "How de do de do?"

Aunt Kate ignored his hand. "Hello," she said coldly.

"Aren't you something, though," he said.

"What exactly?" asked Aunt Kate.

"Ho ho ho," laughed Jake, a bit uncertainly this time.

"Just passing through, are you?" asked Aunt Kate.

"Well, now, I don't know," he said. "I might stop on a while. Get to know my relatives a bit better. I lost my job, you see. Actually, I quit."

"Jake was a tour guide at Mammoth Cave," said my mother.

Aunt Kate snickered. Even I knew that wasn't polite.

"You know why I quit?"

"I can't imagine," said Aunt Kate.

"Bat attack," said Jake.

Aunt Kate snickered again.

"I was just telling the little one here all about it. A bat so big . . ." and he spread his arms.

"Tsk, tsk," said Aunt Kate. "Listen, Jake, I've seen plenty of bats in my day, and I happen to know there are no bats even remotely that large. Not that I care what you think you saw, but there's no sense scaring the little one, is there?"

Since I was the only young one about, I guess they meant me. I wasn't in the least scared.

"Anyhooo," continued Jake, totally unconcerned, "this huge critter swooped down on my head. Tried to tangle himself in my hair. I think he was making for my neck. You know, to bite himself a chunk of flesh and suck my blood. That's what they do."

"How too, too Bela Lugosi," said Aunt Kate. "Will you excuse me, please."

When Aunt Kate left, Jake said, "Nice lady."

"Well, yes," said my mother uncertainly.

"Single?" he asked.

"I think Kate is sort of seeing someone," said Dad. "Come on, Jake, why don't I take you on a drive around town? See the sights."

"Sure thing," said Jake, standing up. "Where I come from, unless you got a ring, you're up for grabs."

"Oh?" tittered my mother. When Mom becomes rattled she drops about 30 points from her IQ.

When they left, I spread my arms and said, *"Sooo big."*

My mom and I laughed.

"I guess I had better think of something to serve tonight," sighed my mother. "Maybe that good cornflake chicken recipe."

"How long is he staying, Mom?" I asked, deftly changing the subject. Thanks to my good work, there was only one box of cornflakes left in the last carton in the garage, but the prospect of being found out was beginning to make me nervous.

"I don't know, Hortense, not long."

"Do we have to have him *and* the weasel pack?"

"Honey, it's important that your sister feel she can entertain her friends here. When I was growing up, my mother and father wouldn't let us have our boyfriends over to the house, and it made things very difficult for me and my sisters."

"But there's nowhere to go but my room, and now I can't even go there."

"I'm sorry, honey, but I just don't see what I can do about it right at the moment," she said.

I went up and knocked on Aunt Kate's door.

"What?" she asked grumpily.

"Can I come in?"

She opened the door and handed me a palmetto fan. "Here," she said. "I bought this downtown." She had one, too, and we sat at her table sipping club soda with raspberry vinegar and fanning ourselves.

"This is really too much," she said. "How do we get rid of this turkey?"

"I think he has romantic designs on you," I said.

"That's what he thinks," said Aunt Kate and passed me a frozen chocolate eclair. "I didn't even bother thawing these," she explained. "In this weather they're much better frozen. Oh, well, I leave for up north this Wednesday."

"Lucky you," I said.

"What have you been up to?" she asked me, languidly fanning herself and looking not very interested, but too hot to do anything but make idle conversation. So I told her all about Virginia and her telescope and my break with Doris. I had hardly seen Aunt Kate for the last few weeks. She had been busy with Old Joe. I had been busy with Virginia. I had given up trying to impress her with my important projects. It didn't seem to matter so much now that I had Virginia to talk to.

"Well, I must say I think Virginia sounds much more interesting than that namby-pamby Doris. It always seemed to me that the thing you enjoyed best about Doris was feeling superior to her," she said, brushing wisps of hair out of her eyes with a graceful hand.

Mom would never have offered such an honest opinion. She would just have said they both seemed like nice girls, or something.

"Are you and Joe going to get married?" I asked.

"I don't know. Why?"

"Well, I would want to know, of course. It would seem awfully dull around here without you."

"Oh, really?" said Aunt Kate and got up to swat a fly with a rolled-up magazine.

"Letitia thinks you would never marry because you are too independent and only wimps gets married."

"I have always valued the insights of fourteen-year-olds," said Aunt Kate in her nastiest way.

When Aunt Kate gets biting, I figure I have worn out my welcome. She can be nice for only so long without cracking.

Every day was hotter and more humid than the next. School let out on Monday, which would have been just jolly except I had no home to relax in. I spent as much time as I could with Virginia but eventually had to face the weasel pack and Jake. On Wednesday, when Aunt Kate was packing her suitcase, I decided to plead with her.

"Take me with you," I said.

"That idiot," said Aunt Kate. "He *pinched* me."

"Where?" I asked.

"Never you mind," said Aunt Kate.

"There, you see?" I said, pressing my case. "How can you leave me alone with him? Dad and Mom are all wrapped up in the baby coming and Letitia has her weasel pack to distract her. I like Virginia, but when I come home, I am all alone."

"All right. For one week," said Aunt Kate. "Go and pack a bag. I'll talk to Ada."

I couldn't believe it. I ran upstairs with wings on my sneakers. When I came down, bag in hand, my mom was tapping her foot and not looking pleased.

"Hortense, do you really want to go up north with Aunt Kate?" she asked.

"Yes," I said. I refrained from pointing out that I had a packed suitcase in my hand.

"Don't you want to be here when the baby comes?"

"It's not coming for two weeks, Mom. I'm only going with Aunt Kate for a week. I'll be back a whole week before the baby gets here."

"Babies don't always arrive when they're supposed to. I'll tell you what really bothers me, Kate—you haven't even got a phone in the cabin. I mean, if we had some way to reach you—"

"You have the phone number of the bar in town."

"Yes, but you know how bad you are at checking for messages there."

"We'll check every day, Ada."

"Oh, all right," said my mother and collapsed bulkily in a chair.

"See you around," I said, giving her a quick peck on the cheek, and I ran to Aunt Kate's car, slammed the door, and sat boldly upright in the bucket seat.

As soon as we hit the highway, Aunt Kate turned some music on on the radio, we opened the car windows, and the wind blew through my hair. I felt free and lighthearted. I had escaped.

Aunt Kate's cabin was beautiful. The smell of pine was thick everywhere. The first day I reveled in catching crayfish and reading on the dock in the sun. Aunt Kate and Joe spent an inordinate amount of time holding hands and looking dreamy-eyed, but I was able to ignore this at first.

On the second day, it occurred to me that I had forgotten to phone Virginia to tell her where I was going and she must be worried sick. Usually we phoned each other about four times a day.

On the third day, I grew a little weary of Aunt Kate's cooking. Even though my mother overdid the cornflake cookery, I had to hand it to her, her meals were delicious and she did most of them from scratch. It had never occurred to me that Aunt Kate didn't know how to cook. We ate entirely out of cans. I couldn't understand how someone who was so into gourmet restaurants could live like this. I was definitely going to buy her a cookbook for her next birthday.

On the fourth day, Joe was over before breakfast and I caught him kissing Aunt Kate when they were supposed to be bringing in wood for the fire. After breakfast, we checked the bar dutifully for messages, as we had done each day, but there was no word. I was kind of sorry. Joe and Aunt Kate had their own routine, and while they were nice enough to me, I felt I had to kind of tippy-toe around them.

I took my cereal out to the dock in the early morning of the fifth day and watched the rosy sun glint across the lake and the mist rise. It had been fun at first to feel like a grownup person in the company of Aunt Kate and Joe. As long as I didn't disturb her writing, Aunt Kate let me do pretty much what I liked without a lot of annoying little rules.

I had never been a houseguest for a whole week before, and it was strange. Even though I had lived with Aunt Kate all my life, this was different. This was her house and I didn't really fit in, not the way I fitted in at home. I found myself being ultra-polite all the time, and that's okay for a day or two, but then it really wears on you.

I thought about Dad and Mom and Letitia, and realized that the thing about families is they're comfortable. You can be a rabbit around the house if you want, I guess, or you can be mad at the rabbits, but no one has to tippy-toe around. But what about this baby? Would it be like having a stranger in the house? A tiny houseguest that would make everyone uncomfortable?

I thought about the weasel pack and the rabbits and Virginia and Doris and Old Joe and even visiting loonies like Jake, and I could see that our family had gotten buffeted around quite a bit this last year. Still and all, the old Hemple spirit was hanging in. "The heck with it," I said to myself, "I've spent all these months worrying and much good it did me. I'll just see what happens. Oh, Hortense Hemple, you wise thing." I smiled benignly at a school of minnows, racing around looking for food. I went back into the cabin to make some toast, convinced that this moment of wisdom had made everything clear and organized. At least for a day or two.

I was finishing my toast when Aunt Kate and Joe came into the kitchen.

"Listen," I said, "do you think we could do something different today?" Meaning, something that doesn't involve kissing.

"Yeah, let's find an auction," said Aunt Kate.

So they hurried through breakfast and we drove off. When we found an auction, it was perfect. There was junk as far as the eyes could see. The auctioneer was talking real fast, just the way they do in the movies. I was looking over the items up for bid when I saw a telescope.

"Boy, if Virginia could see this," I said.

"You can get wonderful bargains at these things," said Aunt Kate.

We settled down in a center row and watched people bid on a whole set of Fiesta ware, then a rolltop desk that was missing the rolling part. Next came a tackle box with a bunch of hand-tied flies that Joe bid on and got for ten dollars, which he said was dirt-cheap. Then the telescope was put on the auction block. I sighed. Two people were bidding halfheartedly and the bidding had only reached twenty-five dollars, which I knew was *nothing*.

"FIFTY DOLLARS," said Aunt Kate in stentorian tones. This was just like Aunt Kate. She was always giving you these sudden shocks. I hoped Joe's heart was real stable.

No one said anything. I gripped the chair in an agony of suspense.

"Fifty dollars, fifty dollars, fifty dollars once, fifty dollars twice." There was a pause. The auctioneer didn't look happy. "Come on, folks, give the little lady some competition. It's the principle of the thing." He shook his head and banged the gavel. *"Sold."*

I sprang up and threw my arms around Aunt Kate. She jumped up and down. "I love getting a bargain!" she whooped.

"Are we giving it to Virginia?" I asked.

"Who else?" she said.

She and Joe and I raced into town to buy ice cream sodas to celebrate. Joe decided he'd rather have a beer and went into the bar, so Aunt Kate and I settled down at the drugstore counter and sipped happily. Joe came in a couple of minutes later with a funny look on his face.

"There's a message for you at the bar," he said to Aunt Kate.

I felt chills run over me.

"Your sister has had the baby," said Joe.

Aunt Kate and I just looked at him. Then we looked at each other.

"You go on to the bar and phone home," said Joe. "I'll settle up things for you here."

Aunt Kate and I walked together into the bar. We didn't say anything to each other. It seemed about ten miles between the drugstore and the bar, even though they were just across the street.

"Can I use the phone?" asked Aunt Kate.

"Course, Kate, help yourself," said the bartender.

Aunt Kate called our house collect and handed me the phone. Letitia answered. Daddy was at the hospital.

"Well, thank God, you finally got the message," said Letitia. "They sent me home to phone the bar and then hang around waiting for you to phone. Now I can get back to the hospital. Oh, boy, what a morning this has been."

"How's Mom?" I asked.

"Oh, she's fine, now. You should have seen her a few hours ago. Actually, I've only been waiting for you to phone for an hour, but it seems like a million years. What a morning!"

"Did you see the baby?" I asked, suddenly jealous that Letitia had been there and I hadn't.

"Are you kidding? I'll tell you the whole story when you get here. Hurry up."

"Just tell me what she's like."

"Oh, my gosh, didn't I tell you? I'm telling you, Hortense,

I can't even think straight, this has been such a morning. It's not a her, it's a *him.*"

"A *him?*" I yelled.

"A hymn?" snapped Aunt Kate, looking suddenly worried and snatching the phone out of my hands. "Letitia, what's going on there?"

Then her face broke into a broad grin. "A boy? Max? That's wonderful. Listen, Letitia, go on back to the hospital and tell your parents we're leaving right this second and should be there in four hours, tops."

She hung up the phone.

We fairly ran across the street, jabbering away like two idiots.

"A boy!" said Aunt Kate.

"She was so sure it was a girl."

"Well, you know your mother. She's always so sure about everything."

"I have a brother."

"They're calling him Max."

"Oh, I think that's a great name for a boy. Don't you think that's a great name for a boy?"

"I've always liked it."

"And Letitia says she wishes I had been there."

We ran into the drugstore and told Joe the happy news. He promised to close up Aunt Kate's cabin for her because we didn't want to bother stopping back there. He said he had errands to do in town and then would find a ride back to his cabin with someone. So we jumped into Aunt Kate's car and sped out onto the highway.

"Let's stop at a toy store on the way home," said Aunt Kate.

"Poor kid doesn't have any boy toys. Oh me, that's so sexist, I don't believe I said that. Let's get him a truck."

"Let's get him a bear," I said. "Let's buy him a big stuffed bear."

"Let's get him a truck and a bear." Aunt Kate giggled.

"Let's get him the biggest bear in the store and the biggest truck," I said.

Then we both giggled.

When we got off the exit ramp going into downtown Riverside, there was a big toy store. We pulled in, and inside we found a huge red truck and a five-foot brown bear. It was just ridiculous. Aunt Kate lugged it to the counter, with me dragging the truck. We couldn't stop laughing maniacally. I'm sure the clerk thought we were nuts. We put them in the back seat and dubbed the bear Manfred. Every so often on the way to the hospital, I would turn in my seat and say, "How are you doing back there, Manfred?" and then Aunt Kate and I would be off in giggles again.

When we got to the hospital, my giggles disappeared and my mouth went dry. Inside was my brother. We walked silently through the green halls and the crush of people, lugging Manfred and the truck. We finally found the nursery. Aunt Kate explained that they kept all the babies there behind glass during visiting hours so they wouldn't get exposed to germs. I wouldn't be able to hold Max until my mom brought him home. In the crowd, with their noses pressed against the glass, the hardest-pressing noses belonged to my sister and dad. Letitia pointed to a little red face that was Max.

"Now there's three of us kids and only two of them," Letitia whispered in my ear and we giggled.

"Don't you think he looks smarter than the other babies?" I said to Dad.

My dad laughed and squeezed my shoulder. "Well, I just hope he turns out as fine as my two girls," he said and then cleared his throat. We were all kind of excited and embarrassed and there were all these other people pushing and shoving to see their babies, so we went down the hall to Mom's room.

"Oh, Hortense," said Mom, "I thought you'd never get here." And she laughed when Aunt Kate and I gave her the truck and the bear.

"Hey, your stomach's all gone," I said and everyone laughed again.

"What time did you have the baby?" asked Aunt Kate when everyone had settled down a bit and found somewhere to sit.

"This morning. I started having the pains at nine o'clock, and Henry had just gone out for milk. But everything started happening too fast. Luckily, Letitia was in the house with me."

"Daddy was at the grocery store, and you know how long that can take," put in Letitia. My dad gets lost and muddled in grocery stores and can take an hour just to get three or four items.

"So I kept telling Letitia to call a taxi," said my mom.

"But I wanted to wait for Dad," said Letitia. "So I kept saying, 'Let's just wait.' And Mom kept panting and then saying, 'Call a taxi or no allowance ever again,' and I kept saying, 'Now, you just hang in there.' "

"And I told her if she didn't call a taxi I was going to have the baby in the house."

"Well, I didn't know enough about babies to tell if she meant it or if she was just panicking. I wished you were home to go on your bike to the store to get Dad," Letitia said, looking at me. "Then Mom stopped panting and started making strange noises."

"So," Mom continued, laughing, "she says to me, 'Think of Lucky, Mom, on a hot day,' and you know, it worked. I thought of that silly dog lying in the sun and I started to pant. Luckily, your dad came back just then and we were off to the hospital, with no time to lose, believe you me."

"What happened to Jake?" I asked.

"He left yesterday," said Letitia.

A nurse stuck her head through the door. "Visiting hours are over," she said.

"Let's take one more look at Max," said Letitia, and everyone filed out, but I lingered behind because I wanted a minute with Mom alone.

"I just wanted to tell you something," I said.

Mom patted the place beside her on the bed and I climbed up.

I didn't really know how to say what I wanted to say. "I think we're going to use your article in our newspaper."

Mom laughed. "Well, thank heavens for that!"

She sat up and gave me a squeeze. "I've just got one question for you."

"Yeah?" I asked.

"What did you do with all the cornflakes?"

"I took them to the food depot," I said.

She nodded. "Well, at least they weren't wasted."

Daddy came back into the room. "Hortense, Letitia is

meeting Kathy downtown, so she's left, and Aunt Kate is waiting for you in the lobby."

"Okay," I said. I slid off the bed and Mom winked at me.

"See you tomorrow," I said. I sneaked back to the nursery and took one more look at Max. All the other babies were sleeping, but he was looking around. I bet he was bored. We'll soon change all that, I thought, then ran down to find Aunt Kate.

"Boy, I'm starved," said Aunt Kate on the way out to the car. So we drove to McDonald's and got burgers. But I couldn't settle down at all and could hardly eat.

I kept thinking about how excited Aunt Kate got when she heard about Max. Come to think of it, it was pretty weird how giddy we had both become. Of course, partially we were just delighted that Mom, ever so certain it would be a girl, was wrong.

"Aunt Kate," I said. "I didn't think you'd be that excited about the baby."

Aunt Kate stopped chewing and fixed me with a steely eye. "Listen, Hortense," she said. "Even though they're not always for the better, changes are always exciting."

"But this was kind of nice."

"Blood is thicker than water," said Aunt Kate, "which is not necessarily convenient, but there it is. That's not to say that I retract anything."

She had lost me there, but I didn't feel like pursuing it. I had had enough for one day.

"I feel like I'm never going to sleep tonight," I said.

"Well, no wonder," she said.

"I can't wait to tell Virginia."

"Let's go home," said Aunt Kate. "And you can call her."

When we got home, I had another thought. I wrote a quick note to Letitia and stuck it on her bulletin board:

> *Dear Fat Hips,*
>   *What are we going to call Max for bulletin board purposes? How about pruneface? Think about it.*
>
>   *Love,*
>   *Medusa*

Then I picked up the phone to call Virginia. She was so excited to hear about Max that we talked about him for ten minutes. "You know, I was worried that my family was going to disintegrate what with the baby and all the new happenings this year," I said. "Well, I don't think our family will fall apart just because it keeps changing."

"After three little brothers, I could've told you that," said Virginia.

"It was quite a discovery . . ." I began and then suddenly remembered something. "Speaking of discoveries," I said, and I told her about my week up north, and when I got to the part about the telescope, she cried.